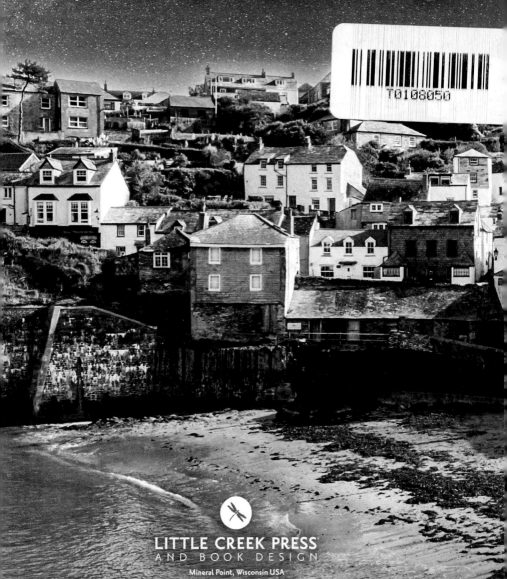

Amy J. Heyman

# Polvenon

LITTLE CREEK PRESS
AND BOOK DESIGN
Mineral Point, Wisconsin USA

Little Creek Press®
A Division of Kristin Mitchell Design, Inc.
5341 Sunny Ridge Road
Mineral Point, Wisconsin 53565

Book Design and Project Coordination:
Little Creek Press

First Edition
January 2018

Printed in Wisconsin, United States of America

For more information or to order books:
email: aheyman@excel.net
or visit www.littlecreekpress.com

Library of Congress Control Number: 2017964695

ISBN-10: 1-942586-32-9
ISBN-13: 978-1-942586-32-6

Cover photo credit: © Andrea Calzona and Standret, Dreamstime.com

## DEDICATION

This book is dedicated to my mother who taught me to love books and shared my passion for all things Cornish.

## ACKNOWLEDGEMENTS

I want to thank Mr. Jim Jewell, Bard of the Cornish Gorsedd, for assisting me in obtaining information about mining in Cornwall in the early 19th century. I also want to thank Mary Cinealis Nohl for encouraging me to finish this novel after 20 years of sitting on Chapter 17! And a big thank you to the Little Creek Press staff for all their hard work in editing and publishing my little book.

# CHAPTER 1

## Cornwall, England – 1827

Emily took one look at the letter in front of her and burst into tears, so happy that she could not express it any other way. It was a letter from her father to the Hopkins School for Girls, requesting that immediate arrangements be made to send Emily home. Since Emily heard the news, she had had a difficult time maintaining the proper demeanor that Dame Hopkins had tried, with little success, to instill in her.

Emily looked upon her stay at Hopkins as a waste of her time. Her instructors did little more than elaborate on the skills and knowledge she had already obtained from Elliot and Norah Trescowe, her adoptive parents. Even though Emily had been at Hopkins for almost two years, she had not made many friends. It seemed as though the other girls were a good deal behind Emily in their studies and so chose to associate with classmates of their own level. Even the relationship between Emily and Dame Hopkins was somewhat reserved. It was for this reason that Emily was quite taken by surprise when Dame Hopkins met her at the coach to say goodbye and wish her well.

The coach ride was almost more than Emily could bear. The seats were hard, wooden planks and the ride so bumpy that, after seven long hours, she thought her back would break. The driver had no consideration for the comfort of his only passenger. Nothing, however, was going to dampen Emily's spirits. The breathtaking landscapes of coastline, dotted with rocky moors were lost on Emily. She was going home! Home through the charming little hamlets, fishermen's coves with quaint little harbors and clusters of thatched cottages, to the village of Polvenon Cove, home to Rumford Inn, the well-respected establishment owned and run by Elliot and Norah Trescowe.

The Trescowes, being childless, had adopted Emily from the orphanage in Tremorna, a town about twenty miles from Polvenon Cove. Emily had been four years old at the time. She still had memories of her life at the orphanage. The outside of the orphanage was grey and dungeon-like as the building had previously been a prison. There were bars on all the windows; Emily used to sit near a bedroom window and wish she had a real home, one where it was warm all the time—and people loved her. All she had ever seen as she peered down, however, was a bleak wilderness.

Suddenly her thoughts were jarred by a loud crack as the rather dilapidated coach leaned dangerously to one side, coming to an abrupt halt and flinging Emily into the opposite seat.

Emily was stunned but managed to get to her feet. Before she could try the door, the ornery driver had opened it and was roughly lifting Emily out of the coach. He did not ask if she was hurt. He seemed more upset that his coach had lost a wheel. His patched coat and shabby appearance almost made Emily feel a bit sorry for him but for his cranky demeanor.

Luckily, Emily was quite all right. As she looked around, she realized they were only about three miles from Polvenon Cove. "If only my trunk weren't so heavy, I could walk the rest of the way," she lamented.

As she pondered her dilemma, the driver of the coach began to shout, in anger, Emily supposed, until she saw the look on his face. She followed the direction of his suddenly eager, bright eyes and saw, to her great relief, a coach coming from the opposite direction. As it drew closer, Emily knew by the shiny black paint and the coat of arms on the door that it was the Polvenon family carriage. She also realized, with some apprehension, that the only passengers it might be carrying would be Philip Polvenon and his son, Alexander. She had not yet met either of them and was not sure she wanted to. Mr. Philip was the landowner of the property on which Rumford Inn stood. He also owned the mines located in and surrounding the town named for his great-grandfather. Emily had heard that he was a penny-pinching tyrant. She knew nothing of his son, Alexander.

The carriage had already stopped, and the footman opened the door, revealing only one passenger. As he stepped from the coach and his body unfolded, Emily noticed how tall he was and how the color of his hair matched that of the carriage. After viewing the dire situation, he walked toward Emily, introduced himself as Alexander Polvenon and offered his assistance. Emily was speechless, mesmerized by the deep blue of his eyes. Before she knew it, Emily was seated in the Polvenon carriage, conversing with Alexander as if she had known him forever.

When they arrived at Rumford Inn, Alexander lifted Emily from the carriage and took her trunk from the footman. "Allow me to escort you to the door," Alexander said, giving Emily one of his disarming smiles.

"Oh no ... please," she stammered, afraid of hurting his feelings. "I mean ... that is not necessary. You see, I need a few moments alone to collect my thoughts before I see my family and friends again. It has been so long since I have been home, and I must try to contain my excitement and act like the lady that I am supposed to have become." Besides, she needed time to think. She was a bit concerned about being called home so suddenly.

Alexander hid a chuckle and bowed politely. "I understand fully Miss Trescowe. I will leave you to prepare in your own way for your homecoming. My only hope is that I may see you again soon."

—◦O◦—

Except for a few noticeable repairs and improvements, Rumford Inn looked the same as when Emily left it. She noticed that her father had patched some of the white plasterwork and replaced the crooked oak timbers of the overhanging upper story. The ground floor had been built of grey stone blocks, the main entrance set in an archway. To the far left, overshadowed by enormous willows, was a private entrance to the rooms of the inn, which were home to the Trescowes.

As Emily stood, happily scrutinizing the cluster of chimneys on the old tiled roof, the immaculate flowerboxes placed under each leaded window, the cobbled paths leading to the inn, the ancient door suddenly swung open, and Elliot and Norah flew to their daughter in a whirlwind of hugs and kisses. After a time, Elliot detached himself, laughing heartily as he watched Norah and Emily try to fit all the events of the past two years into the first five minutes. It still amazed him that Emily reminded him so much of his wife's sister, Margaret, who disappeared one day, never to return.

"Norah," Elliot interjected. "I think that, by the looks of her, Emily could use a home-cooked meal. Why don't we go in and let her freshen up a bit? You two can talk again after she has eaten."

"Oh, Emily!" Norah cried. "I had quite forgotten how hungry and tired you must be. I will go in at once and tell Tudy to cook a nice hot meal for you."

As soon as Norah disappeared, Emily turned to her father. "It is so good to be home, but I cannot help but wonder why you sent for me in the middle of my term. Are you or Mother ill?"

"No, no, my dear. There is nothing for you to worry about. Your mother and I are fine, but we have missed you more than you can imagine, and unless I am mistaken, your letters seemed to indicate the same."

Emily hung her head slightly. "I tried very hard not to let my feelings show in my letters. I am sorry if I have upset you, Papa. It seems that all I ever thought about at school was what you or Mother or Kelly Rose were doing and wishing I could be here."

"You are here now and that is all that matters, Emily." Elliot gave her a quick hug as they walked toward the inn.

# CHAPTER 2

As Philip Polvenon sat in his armchair in front of the vast marble fireplace, studying the remains of his glass of claret, he wondered where Alexander had gone in such a hurry. "It seems that even my own son does not have time for me these days," he sneered. "He is supposed to be learning the responsibilities of running the mine. He is my only son—my only child. Does he not realize what is expected of him? By God, I cannot be expected to oversee this estate and manage the mine as well!"

Overhearing the tail end of his master's grumblings, Benjamin chuckled to himself as he passed the study. "It is good to hear him talk like that," Benjamin mused. "It means he is feeling much his old self again." Neither Benjamin nor Philip's son, Alexander, put much stock in Philip's incessant scolding.

Benjamin, Philip's manservant, was also his lifelong friend and confidante. Benjamin's mother had been Philip's nanny; consequently, Benjamin grew up with Philip and thought of Polvenon Manor as his home. When Benjamin's mother died, he stayed on as Philip's servant. Theirs was a friendship built not so much on love and trust as on loyalty and well-kept secrets.

For reasons other than money—of which Lord Polvenon had an inordinate amount—, the cook, groundskeepers, and other servants had been dismissed years ago, leaving Benjamin the sole caretaker of the Polvenon estate. As a result, the grounds were a shambles with underbrush having taken over the once beautifully kept symmetrical hedges overlooking the gardens, now overgrown with weeds. The outbuildings were abandoned and dilapidated, creating a foreboding and uninviting atmosphere. Philip wanted it this way. He was satisfied with the company of Benjamin and Alexander and, at times, Hugh Spenser, one of Alexander's closest friends. A girl from the village picked up and delivered laundry to Polvenon Manor weekly. There was no need or desire to have any other visitors.

Benjamin didn't mind being the only servant on such a huge estate. He was expected to keep neat and clean only that section of the manor house currently occupied by Philip and Alexander. Meals were not a problem as Benjamin enjoyed cooking. Other than his trips into town to purchase goods and supplies, Benjamin rarely had contact with the outside world.

Benjamin had just finished cleaning up the kitchen for the day when Alexander came in. "I was hoping I could still get a late-night snack, Benjamin. Sorry, I didn't make it for dinner, but Hugh and I helped Mr. Spenser unload a shipment of new books, and it took longer than expected. Is there anything left over from dinner?"

"I've already prepared a plate for you. It is over on the counter. You know, Master Alex, it might have helped your father's disposition to have you here in time for dinner. He was not very happy that you missed mealtime again. After all, it is about the only time he gets to talk to you."

"I know, and I will apologize to him, but he has not been himself lately. He seems so sullen, and it is hard to talk to him when he is that way."

"I think that you will find that he is quite himself again. I overheard him growling about the fact that you are always gone and never around when he needs you."

"That does sound like he's gotten over whatever it was that was upsetting him. Well, Benjamin, thank you for my supper. I will stop in and see what it is he needs me for before I go to my room. Good night, Benjamin. Sleep well."

"Good night, Master Alex, and ...," Benjamin said, but Alex had already gone.

When Alexander had gone into his father's study to speak with him, Philip was asleep in his chair. Alex did not wake him but went to his room instead. He was glad that he did not have to see his father tonight. He had more pleasant things on his mind. Emily Trescowe, for one. He could not forget that long chestnut mane, those deep blue eyes, and that cute dusting of freckles across her nose. She was so beautiful. When she spoke to him in the carriage on the way to her home, he had noticed that her voice had a soothing, calming quality about it. He could have listened to her for hours.

He learned from their conversation that Emily had been adopted when she was a little girl and had grown up at Rumford Inn with the Trescowes. She seemed to have a great longing to know who her real parents were. At this point, she knew nothing at all. She had written to the orphanage in Tremorna to see if they had kept any records of her parentage, but they either did not have or would not release any information to Emily. The Trescowes had also tried over the years to find out about Emily's natural parents but had come up with nothing.

When they had reached Rumford Inn, he had felt a twinge of jealousy over Emily's obvious excitement at being home at last. He could never remember a time in his life that he was actually happy to be home. There must be a lot of love at Rumford Inn and, at that moment, he wished he could be a part of it. Even though Polvenon Manor was home to him, it was not a very happy one. Oh yes, he knew that his father loved him, but it was never shown outwardly. Benjamin also loved him and took good care of both him and his father. But something was missing. When Alex was old enough to understand, Philip had told him that Alexa, Philip's wife, had died giving birth to Alex. Maybe that was it. Maybe having a mother would have made the manor more of a happy, loving home. Alexander drifted off to sleep, dreaming of what might have been.

Philip woke to the smell of thick rashers of bacon frying in the kitchen. He did not remember going to his room the night before. He supposed Benjamin had helped him up the stairs as he did so many times. "What would I do without Benjamin," he thought, as he got dressed and went downstairs to the dining room.

"Good morning, Father." Alex said cheerfully. "I thought you'd sleep late today as it is Sunday."

"Alexander, when have you known me to sleep later than 7:00 a.m.? And why do you sound so chipper today? Were you out with your lady friend ... what's her name ... Winnie last night? That would explain it," he snarled under his breath.

"As a matter of fact, Father, I was with Hugh and Mr. Spenser, helping them unload a shipment of books that came in late yesterday afternoon. It took a lot longer than expected."

"Did you forget that you and I were supposed to discuss the finances of the mine last night? The financial problems are not going to take care of themselves, Alex. I am not getting any younger, and I had hoped that you would have taken more of an interest in my affairs. After all, they will be yours someday."

"I know, Father, and I am sorry about last night. I promise that we will go over the ledgers tomorrow morning."

"What is wrong with today!?" Philip bellowed.

"It is Sunday, and you know that we have never discussed business matters on Sunday, Father." Alex grabbed another rasher from the platter and made a quick exit before Philip could say any more.

# CHAPTER 3

"This is the most delicious meal I've had in two years!" Emily cried. "Tudy remembered all of my favorites." Emily looked up at Tudy's rough-skinned face and smiled. Tudy was the cook at Rumford Inn and was forever complaining about this or that but had a soft spot when it came to Emily. Spread on the table in front of Emily was a roast duck, puffed pastries filled with wild mushrooms and truffles, fresh asparagus, and strawberry tarts for dessert.

"I helped Tudy with the strawberry tarts, dear," Norah said, "and Kelly Rose and Tom Stone picked the wild mushrooms this morning. Honestly, the way those two carry on. They will use any excuse to get off by themselves. Why—"

"Is someone talking about me again?" Kelly Rose chimed as she swept into the kitchen. Kelly Rose was an Irish beauty, her hair the color of coal with fiery highlights, her black eyes twinkling with mischief, and a smile to warm the coldest of hearts. She was hired as the housekeeper when the Trescowes adopted Emily, and she has been Emily's "big sister" and confidante. The minute Kelly Rose set eyes on Tom Stone, the curly-haired barkeep of Rumford Inn, she knew he was the one for her. She loved how protective of Emily Tom was.

"Oh, Kelly Rose! It's so good to see you!" Emily cried as she stood for a long overdue hug. "You are not a very good letter writer, are you? Shame on you!"

"You knew that about me afore you up and left for school, Miss Emily. Saved it all up for just a night like this, I did." Before Kelly Rose left the room, she whispered to Emily, "How about I sneak one of Tudy's tarts up to your room later when you're nice and settled?" Kelly Rose winked at Emily and danced out of the kitchen.

"See what I mean, Emily?" Norah said with a sly grin. "There is definitely something going on between those two. She's been dancing from room to room for the last couple of weeks."

"Tom's been singing Irish ballads while he tends to the customers lately too," Elliot interjected from behind a newspaper. "Before you know it, we'll be losing those two. It's too bad. They are like family."

Emily looked apprehensively at Elliot and then at Norah. "You don't think they would leave Rumford Inn, do you? Why, it's their home. What would we do without them? I don't think I could bear it without Kelly Rose."

"I don't think we have to worry about it for a while, honey," Norah said unconvincingly as she patted Emily's hand.

After a nice hot bath prepared for her by Tudy, Emily put her nightgown on and waited anxiously for Kelly Rose. She would tell her about school, which wasn't much. What she really wanted to talk about was her chance meeting with Alexander Polvenon this afternoon.

"Were you waiting long? I had to help Tom clean tables afore I could come up," Kelly Rose said as she plopped onto Emily's bed, holding a plate of tarts and a glass of milk.

"It seemed to take you forever. How is Tom anyway? I didn't get a chance to say hello to him yet. Is he still as cute as ever?" Emily teased.

"Cuter! Oh, Miss Emily! He is such a good man. And he takes such good care of me. The other day, he said he would like to take care of me always. Just think of it, Miss Emily. Wouldn't it be wonderful?"

"Sounds like a lot has happened between you two while I was gone. It is good that I came home two years early or you might have gone off and married without asking me first!"

"Sure an' you know I would never do anything like that without talking to you first. Besides, Tom really hasn't asked me to marry him, but he certainly has been hinting lately." Kelly Rose took a bite of a tart and said, "Enough of me, young lass. How was school? Did you like it? Did you make new friends? Do you have a boyfriend? Did you—"

"Wait a minute, Kelly Rose. Slow down! I will answer your questions about school, but I will do it quickly, for I have something much more exciting to tell you. School was all right, although it was rather boring. I hardly made any friends, male or female. I was so happy when Dame Hopkins told me I was going home!"

Emily paused and Kelly Rose said, "I'm surprised you are not exhausted after that long, bumpy ride home, Miss Emily. Sure an' I should be letting you get your sleep now, eh?" Kelly Rose teased.

"I am too excited to sleep! Perhaps I won't be able to sleep at all! Oh, Kelly Rose, he is so handsome!"

"Ah, 'tis a boyfriend after all. I was right, wasn't I?"

"No," sighed Emily. "Not a boyfriend. Although he did say he wished to see me again soon."

"Who? Come on, lass. Don't keep me guessing!"

"All right, Kelly Rose, I'll start at the beginning. On my way home from school, the coach I was in broke down about three miles from here."

"Oh, my saints! Are you hurt? Why didn't you tell us? You could have been killed!" Kelly Rose shouted.

"As you can see, I am just fine. A wheel came loose and the coach tipped, but I am all right except for a small bruise on my shoulder. The driver helped me out of the coach, and as I was standing there wondering what I was going to do, another coach came from the opposite direction. It stopped, and you will never guess who stepped out, Kelly Rose. It was none other than Alexander Polvenon himself!"

Kelly Rose gasped. "Oh no, Miss Emily! What did you do?"

"He offered to take me home in his coach. Before I knew it, we were riding toward Polvenon Cove."

"Was Mr. Polvenon the only other passenger? Oh, Miss Emily. I do not like the sound of this at all."

"Yes, Mr. Polvenon and I were alone in the coach, but what was I supposed to do? I didn't know when another coach would happen to pass by. I couldn't carry my heavy trunk for three miles. I was very thankful that he offered to take me home, although I was hesitant. Kelly Rose, what do you know about the Polvenons?"

"Just what everyone else does—that Master Philip is a wretched beast and a tyrant, although he wasn't always. I've heard it said that years ago when Master Philip was married, he was the nicest man. His wife, however, died in childbirth, and he wasn't quite the same after that. Years later he met and fell in love with a woman. She did not love him; in fact, she despised him. Alas, she only had eyes for another. They loved each other and were going to get married. Mr. Philip was insanely jealous and did everything in his power to put a stop to the relationship between her and her lover. Then suddenly, they both disappeared. No one has seen them since."

"What a sad story, Kelly Rose. So, no one has ever found them?"

"No, lass. Every effort was made to find them, but with no success. 'Tis just assumed they ran off together to get away from Philip Polvenon's twisted rage. 'Twas almost sixteen years ago now, Miss Emily."

"Kelly Rose," Emily interrupted, "Why did you gasp when I mentioned Alexander Polvenon? Is it because you think he is like his father?"

"I don't know, Miss Emily. Alexander never had a mother and was brought up by Philip and his manservant. It could not have been a very happy upbringing. But then, Philip Polvenon might have treated his own flesh and blood differently than he treats the rest of this town. I suppose 'twas the fact that you mentioned the Polvenon name that startled me."

"From my brief conversation with Alexander Polvenon, I found him to be a most pleasant man. He certainly knew his manners and treated me with the greatest respect. What's more, he was friendly and interesting to talk to."

"You said afore that he wants to see you again. Do you think 'tis a good idea? The townspeople will talk, you know. Pardon me for saying so, Miss Emily, but the Polvenons would consider the Trescowe family … a bit beneath them. I would be more comfortable if I knew more of Mr. Alexander's character and motives afore you see him again."

Emily sighed. "Well, Kelly Rose, I don't think I will be seeing him in the near future. You are right. Our lives are so different. When would I ever get the opportunity to see him again even if I wanted to?"

"I think 'tis time you got to bed, young lady. We'll have plenty of time to talk now that you're home. Oh, Miss Emily, 'tis good to have you here again. Good night, lass."

"Goodnight, Kelly Rose." Emily fell asleep as soon as Kelly Rose put out the lamp.

# CHAPTER 4

As Philip and Alexander passed the auction site, tributors were bidding against each other for pitches. Alexander had attended these auctions since he was a boy, and they never ceased to amaze him. These men, some of them boys, would offer to work a pitch for 60 percent of the worth of the ore they extracted. The lord of the manor took the other 40 percent as rent. Tributors had to pay for their own expenses, which included anything from candles and tools to food for their families. Sometimes they had to borrow money from the mine just to exist until the following month. "It is a hard life," thought Alexander. But he had a great respect for the people who worked in his father's mines. They had a proud spirit and a common bond that Alexander was sometimes envious of.

While Philip spoke with the mine captain, Alexander walked over to one of the dressing floors. Women and children did most of the work here. The younger children picked the ore-bearing rocks up from the washing tables and took them to be crushed. The tin and rock were then separated and broken up into gravel by being hammered and stamped. This process was done by the older girls who were called bal maidens. They wore thick aprons to protect their clothing from the dust. Alexander was noticing a particularly pretty maiden when Philip approached him from behind. "Alex, how in God's name are you ever going to learn anything if you don't stick by me? I wish you would pay as much attention to me as you do to every blushing maid who happens to cross your path."

"You are exaggerating again, Father." Alex sighed, raising his eyes.

"Am I?" Philip sneered. "You haven't heard a word anyone has said to you for the past few days. Now, I would like you to come with me to the storehouse to check with the man in charge of supplies."

As Philip and Alexander walked toward the storehouse, all hammering on the dressing floor stopped. It was a silence reserved for dinnertime and the end of a workday. Something was wrong. Alexander turned and saw that the bal maidens had gathered together at one end of the dressing floor; some were kneeling beside a girl who had fallen. Before Philip could stop him, Alexander ran over to the scene, pushed the maidens out of the way and gently picked the girl up in his arms. He brought her to a spot where a soft patch of grass grew and lay her there. No one followed him, but all looked on with wonder. It was not every day that a lord of the manor or his son was seen showing signs of compassion for a common mine worker.

Alexander noticed a rather large, jagged cut on the side of the girl's head. It looked as though she might have fallen on a sharp rock. "She looks so pale," Alexander thought. As he pushed back a golden lock from her forehead, a little girl came up beside him. "Will she be a'right, do 'ee think, sir?"

"Well, little girl, I think she will be just fine. Do you know her?"

"She is my sister, sir. Her name is Joanna—Joanna Simmons."

"And what is your name?" Alex asked, noticing that she had the same golden curly hair as her older sister.

The girl looked shyly at her bare feet and whispered a barely audible, "Katherine, sir."

"Has your sister been ill as of late, Katherine?"

"Oh, no, sir." Katherine said quickly, her big blue eyes fearful as she looked into his. "T'ain't never happened afore, sir, honest."

Alex wondered why Katherine seemed so afraid. It seemed as though she was trying to hide something. "Where do you live, Katherine? Is it far from here?"

"We live in Helsted, sir. Our mammy and us moved there when Papa was killed," Katherine explained quietly, her head bowed.

"Did your papa work in the mine?" Alex asked hesitantly, knowing what the answer would be.

" 'E were killed in the mine, sir. 'Tis why Mama wanted to move away from 'ere."

Alex winced. He should be used to it by now—men and boys killed in mining accidents or from black lung, but it still affected him deeply. "Do you walk all the way from Helsted to the mine every day, Katherine?"

"Yes, sir. Sometimes Joanna carries me part of the way, but I think I'm getting too big for that now." Katherine smiled.

"Helsted was only two and a half miles from Polvenon Cove, but that is a long way for a little girl," Alex thought. Just then Joanna moaned, and Alex saw that she was trying to sit up.

"Wh-what happened?" Joanna stammered as she tried to focus her eyes on Katherine.

"Ye fainted again!" Katherine whispered to Joanna so that Alex wouldn't hear her.

"How do you feel, Joanna?" Alex said as he knelt beside her. "Do you think you can walk?"

"Oh, aye, thank ye, sir," she said, trying to sound and act as though she was just fine. "I will be all right, sir. I should have eaten breakfast this morning, but we would have been late for work. If I eat my dinner now, I should be able to go back to work soon." Joanna started to get up but found she could not without Alex's help.

"I do not think you will be working anymore today, Joanna. Come, I will take you home," Alex said, and carried her to his horse. "It may be a bumpy ride, but it is better than walking."

"Oh no, sir! I ... I could not. T'ain't right." Joanna said, but Alex had already placed her in front of him on his horse.

"It would not be wise for you to walk home, Joanna. Not today. Come, Katherine!" he shouted to the little girl. "We will go slowly so that you can walk along beside us. I would let you both ride, but I am afraid you are not strong enough to hold on to your sister should she faint again."

As they left for Helsted, Philip looked on, shaking his head in disgust. "What kind of son have I raised. A ninny. What a fine show he is putting on," Philip muttered to himself. "Get on with your work!" he shouted to the maidens as he stomped to the storehouse.

Upon reaching Joanna and Katherine's home, Alex observed that it was no more than a hovel. Two little children were chasing each other around the grounds, and a goat was tied to a tree behind the tiny cottage. The children wore no more than very thin cotton dresses, but they were clean and seemed engrossed in their play. As Alex slid off his horse, he took Joanna in his arms.

"Really, Master Polvenon," Joanna protested. "I can walk by myself. I feel much better now, thank ye."

Katherine had gone ahead to the house to tell her mother what had happened and to prepare her for the shock of an encounter with Alexander Polvenon. "Does 'e suspect anythin' then, Katherine?" Mrs. Simmons whispered, fear in her voice for her daughter and for what could happen.

"No, Mum. 'E's a nice man, Mum. 'E's brought Joanna home on 'is own horse. Shoulda seen 'er, sittin' pretty like in front of 'im ...," Mrs. Simmons shushed Katherine. She didn't want to hear that. No daughter of hers would be caught dead with a Polvenon. However, she knew that the Polvenon miners had just witnessed a display that would be talked about for months to come. "Oh, my Lord!" she groaned.

Mrs. Simmons masked the seething hatred she felt as Joanna walked in the front door with Alexander at her side. "Joanna, are ye all right?" she asked, trying to keep her voice steady.

"Yes, Mum," Joanna murmured. She knew what her mother was going through at that moment.

Mrs. Simmons looked stonily at Alexander. "Thank ye for your help Master Polvenon. I am sure that ye have more important things to tend to, so ye might as well be on your way. We can take care of our own just fine."

Alexander could feel the tension in the room. Not wanting to make things any more difficult for Joanna and Katherine, he nodded toward Mrs. Simmons, turned and left without saying a word.

Alexander arrived home very late that night. He had stopped to visit with Hugh Spenser and his father, consciously avoiding a confrontation with his own father. Morning would be soon enough for that. Alex had enough to think about tonight. He thought he knew all there was to know about the foul conditions the miners lived in, but he was shaken by what he saw today. He knew what that disabling poverty did to most people. It made them bitter and old before their time. Yet the Simmons family seemed happy and content with their lot, although Mrs. Simmons seemed rather unfriendly toward him. Katherine had mentioned that her father had been killed in the mines and that was why they had moved from Polvenon Cove to Helsted—to be far away from the memories of that awful day. Alex shuddered to think what it would be like to live as the Simmons did—not knowing when or if they were getting their next meal; walking two and a half miles to work the mines each day; the livelihood of two younger ones and their mother at home weighing heavily on their shoulders. "They are so young," Alex thought, and his heart went out to them. What could he do? He alone could do nothing of value for these people. There were so many like them. As Alex pondered these things, he made a promise to himself that he would speak to his father about it in the morning, come what may.

"I do not know what ye were thinkin', Joanna!" Mrs. Simmons cried.

Katherine quickly came to her sister's defense. "She weren't thinkin' nothin', Mum. She were real sickly, n' Master Polvenon was there afore we knew it. T'wasn't 'er fault she took sick. I were right grateful that 'e offered to take 'er home. Couldn't have done it by meself, Mum."

"Oh hush, Katherine. Let Joanna speak for 'erself. After all, it were she who made a spectacle of 'erself. Lettin' 'erself n' us in for a lot of trouble, I reckon. Can't much good come of this, now can it?"

Joanna felt sick again. She leaned back on her cot and closed her eyes. "Please, Mum. Try to understand. I 'ad no choice. It all 'appened so fast. T'were no 'arm done, Mum. Wagging tongues never 'urt anyone." Joanna rolled over and curled up. She didn't want to have to explain anymore. She just wanted to sleep.

Mrs. Simmons was quiet for a long time before she whispered, "She's right, ye know, Katherine. Seems that Master Polvenon don't know more than it were just a little faintin' spell. That's all that matters. T'will be all right, Katherine. Go to bed now."

# CHAPTER 5

Emily spent her sixteenth birthday with her parents, Kelly Rose, Tom Stone, Tudy, and anyone else who happened to stop at the inn during the celebration. Knowing Emily's love of books, Elliot and Norah had given her money to spend at Spenser's Bookstore. Kelly Rose had knit a pair of new gloves and a matching scarf for her. Tudy made an apple crisp for the party and promised Emily a batch of shortbread cookies. Tom Stone was singing Emily's favorite Irish ballad:

> *"If I had money enough to spend*
>
> *And leisure time to sit awhile*
>
> *There is a fair maid in this town*
>
> *That sorely has my heart beguiled."* [1]

Tom soon forgot that he was singing to Emily and turned his attention to Kelly Rose who was standing in the doorway looking pretty even with her apron hanging askew and her hair mussed from the heat of the kitchen.

*"Her rosy cheeks and ruby lips*

*I own she has my heart in thrall*

*Then fill to me the parting glass*

*Good night and joy be with you all."* [1]

[1] *Moore, Thomas. "The Parting Glass"*

"How lucky Kelly Rose is to have someone like Tom," Emily mused. "I hope I get that lucky someday." Emily's mind wandered inadvertently to the week before, when she was escorted home by Alexander Polvenon. How handsome he was. And his manners were impeccable. Emily wondered how such a nice person could emerge from the horrible upbringing he must have had—his father being the ogre that he is.

Emily was startled out of her thoughts by the booming voice of Mr. Terwilliger. " 'Appy birthday to ye, missy! Damned if ye don't look prettier ever time I see ye. 'Tis a wonder why ye haven't off 'n wed by now."

Emily blushed but smiled politely and offered him a piece of apple crisp. Mr. Terwilliger was a salesman who traveled from village to village. When in Polvenon Cove, he frequented Rumford Inn, telling tales and searching out bits of news he could elaborate on in the next town. He wore a tattered old hat and a long shabby coat. Everyone listened to him because, most of the time, his information was at least partially true.

"Did ye all hear the latest?" Terwilliger shouted to anyone who would listen. "One of they Simmons girls took sick at the mine yesterday—kind of swooned like and fell over as if dead to the world. T'wasn't the first time either, I hear."

"One of the Simmons girls!" Emily cried, jumping out of her chair. "Was it Joanna, Mr. Terwilliger?"

"Don't know 'er name, missy, but she be the older of the two."

"Oh, my God," whispered Emily. "I knew something was wrong when she didn't come today. She has never missed one of my birthdays since we've know each other." Emily turned to Norah. "Oh, Mother, I must go see Joanna. I have to know that she is all right."

"Yes, of course," Norah agreed. "I'll get your father to take you there. It is getting rather late in the day, and I would feel better if he went with you." Norah left the room to find Elliot.

"Ye ain't heard the best of it, missy. It were none other than young Master Alex who took 'er home on 'is own horse. Shoulda seen 'is father lookin' after 'im with such a look of disgust like I never seen afore."

"Oh, Mr. Terwilliger! Was Joanna all right? Could you see if she was all right?" Emily asked anxiously.

"Aye, missy, she come to after a spell, she did. Now don't ye worry so, Miss Emily. Young Master Alex will see to it she be proper taken care of." Mr. Terwilliger gave Emily a wink and shuffled to the bar to get a pint of ale.

Elliot had entered the room as Mr. Terwilliger was finishing his tale. "Emily, are you sure you still want to go to Helsted today? It is getting late, and it sounds to me as if Joanna will be fine. You've had a big day, and I think it would be best if we waited 'til morning. I'll have Tudy pack some of those shortbread cookies to take to Joanna and, after your visit, I can drop you off at Spenser's store on the way back so you can spend your birthday money."

Emily nodded. She was too tired to argue, and he was right. It did sound as if Joanna would be all right, at least for now. "All right, Father, and thank you so much for the party. I'd like to say goodnight to everyone before I go up to bed." She gave her father a fierce hug, so thankful that she had such wonderful parents.

Emily could not sleep. She was worried about Joanna and her family. Emily had known Joanna Simmons ever since Emily was adopted by Elliot and Norah and came to live in Polvenon Cove. She was four years old at the time. Joanna was her first friend in this new town. At that time Mr. and Mrs. Simmons and their two daughters, Joanna and Katherine, lived in Polvenon Cove and Mr. Simmons worked in the mines. Two years ago, he was killed in a mine explosion. It was a horrible death and one that Mrs. Simmons could not accept. She took her family to live in Helsted to try to forget what had happened—to be as far from the mines as possible. Joanna and Katherine tried to find work in Helsted, but there just wasn't anything that would support a family of five. Mrs. Simmons was forced to send her daughters to Polvenon Cove to work on the dressing floor of the same mine which took her husband. Thus, for the last two years, Joanna, now sixteen years old, and Katherine, nine years old, walked two and a half miles to Polvenon Mine every day except Sundays. Sometimes, if they were lucky, a cartload of miners passing by would give them a ride.

Joanna had always had a weak constitution. She could never do as much work or have as much fun as the rest of the children. When she got too heated, she had difficulty catching her wind, which would usually cause a terrible coughing spell. Joanna had fainted before, but Emily knew that this was the first time it had happened while she was working at the mine. Emily also knew what this could mean to Joanna and her family. Joanna could lose her job at the mine. Philip Polvenon had no sympathy for "weaklings," male or female. Many miners had lost their jobs, with no compensation, because of illness.

It still puzzled Emily how Alexander Polvenon could be such a kind, helpful man when his father was such an insensitive, unfeeling beast. Mr. Terwilliger had said that it was Alexander who took Joanna home. Emily tried to imagine what it would be like to have Alexander's arms around her, as they must have been around Joanna, on their ride to Helsted. With a sudden twinge of jealousy, Emily finally fell into a troubled sleep.

# CHAPTER 6

Benjamin had been up since dawn cleaning out the fireplaces and making breakfast for Philip and Alex. He had known to draw a hot bath for Master Alex, as Alex had come in too late the night before to have had one then. It was when Alex stood up from the bath to dry himself that he looked out the back window and noticed Benjamin walking toward the kitchen door of the manor with what looked like a tray in his hands. Puzzled, Alex questioned him about it at breakfast. Benjamin hesitated, looking a bit startled, then laughed nervously and said that there were scraps left from his breakfast, and he had gone out to feed the birds. "If it were up to you, Benjamin, you would feed every living creature within ten miles of here." Philip teased as he entered the dining room, winking at Benjamin and turning an icy glare toward his son.

"Well, Alexander. And what living creatures will you come to the aid of today, hmm? Another damsel in distress, perhaps?"

Alex was used to this kind of behavior from his father. He ignored Philip's remark and began to explain his concern about the living conditions of the miners who worked for him. "Have you ever actually seen how these people live, Father? In broken down cottages with little food or clothing to keep the cold out, that's how! If you don't give a damn about the miners and their families, I would at least think that you would be concerned about what other mine owners are saying about the way you treat your workers."

"That's enough!" his father roared. "Watch your tongue, boy! And don't try to tell me how to run my business! Not until you show some interest in it yourself."

Alex stared at his father. It was no use. All his life Alex had tried to live up to his father's expectations. Well, no more. He was through biting his tongue, looking the other way when something was done that he didn't like. He didn't have to work for his father. There were other jobs in Polvenon Cove—in the surrounding villages for that matter. He had no strong ties to his father or his business. "It is about time I take matters into my own hands," thought Alex. He stood up and left the dining room without saying a word.

"You better think about what I said, boy!" Philip shouted after him. "It's time you earned your money!" Philip turned to Benjamin. "Next time you slip up like that, Benjamin, I might not be here to cover for you." Philip stomped from the room, leaving a bewildered and shaken Benjamin behind.

# CHAPTER 7

"'Tis Miss Emily, Mum! Come to see Joanna!" Katherine shouted as she ran out to greet Emily.

"Hello, Katherine. It's been awhile since I've visited. You're growing like a weed!" Emily exclaimed. "How is Joanna, Katherine? Was she hurt very badly? I do hope she's up to having company."

"Oh, Miss Emily! Joanna will be glad to 'ave company, 'specially 'tis you." Katherine grinned. "She's doing all right now. She's getting lots of rest. Mum's worried though. Says something's not right with Joanna."

"Has the doctor been to see her?" Emily asked, knowing full well he had not.

"No, Miss Emily. Mum says the less people find out 'bout this, the better. Oh, 'ere comes Joanna. She's fresh up from a nap, so she'll be able to visit with you awhile now." Katherine jumped off the stoop of the rickety porch, waved to Emily, and sped down the path to play with her friends, waving to Elliot who was sitting in the cart, reading a newspaper, while Emily visited Joanna.

"I could use some of that girl's energy," Joanna said wanly. "Come up and sit in this chair next to me, Emily. It seems like ages since I've seen you. I'm so sorry that I missed your birthday party. I would have come, but Mum put a stop to it."

"Don't be silly!" Emily scolded. "You were there in spirit. That's all that matters. Besides, I'm getting too old for birthday parties."

"But Emily. Your sixteenth is your last official party."

"Well, I brought you some of Tudy's shortbread cookies. I know how much you like them." Emily could not take her eyes off Joanna. It had been about a month since she'd last seen her.

"Mrs. Simmons is right," Emily thought. "There is something seriously wrong." Joanna's skin was ashen, and she had lost weight. She seemed to have aged a great deal, and her voice was hoarse as if she had been coughing a lot. Trying not to show too much concern, Emily asked, "How are you feeling, Joanna? Mr. Terwilliger told me that you had fainted on the dressing floor. Do you think it was from the heat?"

"I don't know, Emily," Joanna said in a barely audible voice. "It could 'ave been the heat. Maybe I was working too hard."

"Well, it was very good of Mr. Polvenon to have seen to it that you were taken care of properly, don't you think, Joanna?" Emily asked.

"Oh, Emily!" Joanna exclaimed. "He were that nice, he was! It were all done proper and respectful-like, even though there's some that'll make more of it than 'twas. Oh, but he is an 'andsome one, Emily. And such manners for bein' his father's son an' all. As sick as I was feelin', I felt a bit of a princess when he swept me up in his arms and rode away with me like that. T'will most probably be the high point in me life, Emily, leastways so far 'tis."

Emily couldn't help but notice a new excitement in Joanna's voice and manner. The tiny twinge of jealousy that goaded Emily the night before hit her full force as she listened to Joanna go on about her adventure. She kept putting herself in Joanna's place—on Alexander's horse and in his arms ...

"It were really rather awkward at first, Emily. I mean, what does someone like me have to say to Master Polvenon that would be of any interest to a man like 'im? But, you know, he talked about such nice simple things—like how blue the sky was and how pretty the primroses were wi' the sun shinin' on 'em—and how cute Katie looked skipping 'long side of us like a little filly. He were that easy to talk to, Emily. Really very nice—not all airs like 'is father—not at all."

Joanna began to cough, a loud and persistent cough, unlike any Emily had ever heard before. It startled her. Quickly, Emily gave her handkerchief to Joanna as Joanna began to choke, tears running down her cheeks as she struggled to breathe. Mrs. Simmons came running and began rubbing Joanna's back, trying to calm her cough somehow. When it subsided a bit, Joanna took the kerchief from her mouth, and Emily stifled a gasp when she saw the small bloodstains there. Grabbing the kerchief from her daughter's hand, a very shaken Mrs. Simmons said, "I'm so sorry; I'll 'ave this washed an' cleaned up for you, Miss Emily. I think 'tis time Joanna rested now. I'll send Katie to come an' help you to bed, Joanna." Before Emily could say anything to her, Mrs. Simmons turned and rushed into the house. Joanna tried to talk, but Emily immediately pleaded with her friend to keep quiet, as that was the best thing for her right now. With Katie's help, Emily took Joanna to her bed. When she bent down to kiss her cheek and say goodbye, Joanna had already fallen asleep, her breathing very raspy and uneven.

Emily stepped onto the porch and found Mrs. Simmons crying and Elliot trying to comfort her. "Is there anything I can do, Mrs. Simmons?"

Emily asked quietly. "Would you like me to get the doctor?" Joanna's mother shook her head vehemently.

"No, Miss Emily! No doctors! Never no doctors! No matter what 'appens. The best thing you can do for 'er, miss, is to keep quiet about this. Please, miss, for all our sakes!"

Emily couldn't sleep again that night. Why was Mrs. Simmons so strongly against consulting a doctor about Joanna's condition? What was she afraid of? How could Emily just do nothing about this when Joanna was her best friend? Emily finally decided she had to talk to someone about this. She would talk to Kelly Rose about it.

Emily eventually drifted off to sleep, dreaming of wild horses and bloodstained primroses.

# CHAPTER 8

Alexander was having dinner with the Spensers this evening. He had always enjoyed their company. Hugh Spenser was his best friend. He and his father, Creighton, owned the bookshop in Polvenon Cove and kept to themselves. Hugh was the shop's bookkeeper, and because his taste in reading material differed so from his father's, both poured through the many catalogs of books, and as a result, Spenser's Bookshop was known for its versatility. Alex was looking forward to a quiet evening at the Spenser home. Whenever things were troubling him, he knew that if he talked them over with Creighton and Hugh, they would be able to give him diverse insights, and many times he came away with a different outlook. Well, things were certainly bothering him tonight.

After a splendid meal of roast beef, new potatoes, and fresh leeks in butter sauce, Alex and the Spensers retired to the small, but cozy sitting room, warmed by soft candlelight and a fire in the grate. It was certainly not what one would expect of a typical sitting room; it was filled with oversized velvet chairs of deep wintergreen with large matching ottomans. The walls were a deep shade of rich cherry wood, and a Turkish rug of deep reds and purples lined the small room almost wall to wall. In place of the conventional English countryside scene, above the mantle was an oil painting of a bespectacled, balding man seemingly engrossed in a large volume by the light of a single wick. As he did on his many visits to this room, Alex chuckled to himself at the similarities of the man in the painting to Creighton Spenser, both physical and in character.

"So, Alex, I can see that something is on your mind this fine evening," Hugh's father said as he poured each of them a glass of port. "I'll take a gander that it has something to do with a woman. Am I right?"

"Not a woman." Alex sighed. "Women in general, I think."

"Oh, well!" exclaimed Hugh teasingly. "I think we're in for a long night."

"Well, now this should prove an interesting topic since none of us in this room have had any relationship with a woman—mother, wife, daughter, or otherwise—for quite a while. Are you talking about a specific category, Alex?" Creighton asked, seeming genuinely willing to discuss this fascinating subject.

"None. Not yet anyway," Alex said as he stood up, looking for all the world as if he were going to give a formal speech. "You both know how I feel about the mines. God, you've heard me spout about that until I'm blue in the face. Today something happened that only heightened my intense dislike—hatred more like—of the harsh treatment of the workers. A young girl, Joanna, I think her name is, fainted on the dressing floor today.

"Is she all right, Alex?" Hugh asked. "Did you assist her?"

"Yes, I did, which vexed my father immensely!" Alex laughed bitterly.

"I have already heard of your heroism from a number of customers today, Alex. The story of your rescue of the damsel in distress gave rise not only to the village gossips but to your father's temper as well,"

Creighton said in a serious tone, knowing firsthand the wrath of Philip Polvenon. "Do you think it was wise to come to the girl's aid, knowing how it would anger your father?"

"What would you have had me do, Mr. Spenser? Leave her there on the dressing floor?" Alex demanded, sounding a bit like his father at that moment. "I'm sorry, Mr. Spenser. I know what you are saying. My father's anger does not bother me in the least. What bothers me is what I saw when I took Joanna home. I saw four mouths waiting to be fed. Joanna has a younger sister, Katie, who also works at the mine. Their income is all that they have to live on. There are two younger ones and the mother at home—if you can call that tumbledown shack a home. Their father was killed in the mine explosion two years ago. Sound familiar? When is this going to stop? My God, how can people let this go on? I feel so helpless!" Alex plopped in a chair, throwing his legs up on an ottoman, closing his eyes as if to block out the scene he witnessed today.

Hugh stood up and walked to the fireplace, staring into the fire. "I know you don't want to hear this, Alex, but the only way you can change any of this is to work side by side with your father. Learn enough about the mines to begin making small concessions, and maybe someday the miners will be lucky enough to work under your leadership."

Alex grunted. "You're right, Hugh, I don't want to hear this. However, I agree that there is no other way. But God grant me patience; I don't know if I can do it."

"You've got to try, Alex," Creighton comforted. "We will be here to lend our support whenever and however you may need it." Hugh nodded in agreement. "Let's just pray that the girl will be all right. Alex, to change the subject a bit, do you have any other quandaries about women?"

"Oh, yes!" Alex exclaimed. "On to a more pleasant topic. Miss Emily Trescowe, to be precise."

"Emily Trescowe! I know her!" Hugh cried. "She's one of our regulars and, I should also add, one of our favorite customers. How and where did you happen to meet her?"

"A few miles outside of Polvenon Cove. The coach she was returning from school in had lost a wheel. She was in quite a dilemma as she had quite a few parcels and a very heavy trunk." Alex couldn't help but smile as he thought of Emily standing there in the middle of the road, stomping her feet and making faces at the broken-down vehicle.

Creighton interrupted his thought. "I suppose you thought it only proper to give the poor lady a lift? Did it also occur to you that you may have, at the same time, jeopardized the girl's reputation? I assume she accepted your offer?"

Alex replied rather testily. "I couldn't just let her stand there until a respectable old maid happened to be riding by, or possibly a thief, or worse."

"Come on now, Alex. I didn't mean anything by what I said. I guess you're right. What else could you have done under the circumstances?" Creighton said while tamping fresh tobacco into his pipe. "Well, I gather from your tone of voice that the ride back to Polvenon Cove was in pleasant company?"

"Yes, it was," Alex sang. "Very pleasant indeed. She was like a breath of springtime air—so easy to talk to."

"And to listen to," Hugh interjected. "I know that myself because I love to hear the excitement in her voice whenever she tells me about a new book she's heard about or one she's just read."

"I understand that her parents own Rumford Inn," Alex said. "I've never frequented the place myself, but I've heard that it is quite respectable."

"Oh yes. Indeed, it is. I've been there myself on occasion," Creighton said, much to the surprise of his son, who thought that his father never went anywhere. "The Trescowes are not her real parents, however. They adopted her from the Tremorna Orphanage when she was a little girl."

"Do either of you know anything of her real parents?" asked Alex.

"Not really, Hugh sighed. " Mrs. Trescowe once told me that Emily has always questioned the whereabouts of her real mother and father. Mr. Trescowe has done some investigating but has only found that they are both presumed dead. No other information was available from the orphanage. The girl has not lacked for anything though, Alex. She has had a wonderful childhood and seems to have a real sense of family with the Trescowes. She is also very close with their housekeeper, Kelly Rose."

"Do you know," exclaimed Hugh, "now that you mention it, Miss Trescowe was in our shop just the other day asking if we had any information on the orphanage in Tremorna and if we had a map or could tell her how to get there."

"Hmm," Creighton said wonderingly as Alex looked up, rather puzzled himself.

"It seems as though her curiosity has not yet been satisfied," Alex said. "Did you have any information you could give her, Hugh?"

"Not really, although I did tell her to come back on Friday as I might be able to dig up a map for her by then."

Alex's countenance brightened suddenly. "Friday, you say? Well then, I guess I'll see you on Friday. Great meal, as usual, Mr. Spenser. I better be going. I left my father in rather a huff this morning."

The Spensers exchanged winks as they said their goodbyes to Alex.

# CHAPTER 9

A soft knock on her bedroom door brought Emily's nose out of a book just long enough to say, "Come in." Kelly Rose entered quietly, watching Emily turn the pages slowly, wonder and awe in her eyes. "Oh, Kelly Rose! Look at my wonderful new book! I purchased it with my birthday money yesterday, and it's full of wildflowers—huge sketches with the names and descriptions written below! Did you ever see anything so beautiful?"

"Aye, miss, I have. 'Tis the look on your face right now tops any picture in that book." Kelly Rose began to make the bed and fluff the pillows. "Well, miss, thought as I'd take a bit of a break from my work now, but I can come back later."

"Oh no, Kelly Rose. I've been waiting for you to have some free time so I could talk to you about something," Emily replied as she lay her book aside.

"Aye, 'tis what I thought, miss. Last evening, you was no verra talkative when you came home. That's not like you, miss, pardon my saying so." Kelly Rose winked at Emily as a grin spread across Emily's face.

"Sometimes I think you know me better than I do, Kelly Rose. It's about Joanna."

"The Simmons girl?" Kelly Rose asked as she sat on the edge of the bed.

"Yes, the oldest one," Emily sighed. "She is not well at all. What puzzles me is that neither she nor her mother want to get a doctor in to see her. She's so pale, Kelly Rose. And she is so very weak. She can barely talk without coughing."

"Miss Emily," Kelly Rose spoke wonderingly, "do ye happen to know if she has coughed up any blood?"

At this, Emily jumped up, concern written all over her face. "Oh, Kelly Rose! Yes! Yes, she did while I was there, in fact. But, Kelly Rose, what can that mean? Is she going to die? She just can't die!" Emily stared at Kelly Rose, tears forming on her cheeks. Kelly Rose knew only too well what might be ailing Joanna. She saw her brother, Ian, languish and cough his way toward death. She remembered how she thought his rosy cheeks were a sign of returning health, but they were, in fact, an indication that the fever had come upon him. She knew that the poor living conditions of the Simmons family were just right for breeding these types of lung diseases. The swooning faints that Joanna experienced were a sign that the disease had progressed and that the end might be near.

"Well, Miss Emily," Kelly Rose said quietly as she put her arm around Emily to comfort her. "I am not a doctor, but I've heard and seen too many things in my lifetime to know that your friend is very ill. Spitting up blood is a bad sign, and even if they was to get a doctor in to look at her, Miss Emily, 'tis likely too late for him to do much good for her now."

Emily tore herself away from Kelly Rose and flung herself face down on the bed, sobbing hysterically. "No, it cannot be!"

Kelly Rose sat on the edge of the bed. "You have been a good friend to her, miss. 'Tis what she needs right now. T'will be of comfort to her knowing you are there for her."

"Oh, Kelly Rose," Emily cried as she sat up and hugged her tightly. "You always know the right thing to say. Thank you. I'll try my best."

"Will ye be all right, miss?" Kelly Rose asked.

"Yes, I will be fine. Thank you," Emily said, drying her eyes and rising from the bed. She walked over to the window and as Kelly Rose was about to leave, asked, "Kelly Rose, when is Tom Stone going into Tremorna next?"

"Ah, well, miss. He only goes that distance for certain supplies and that would be 'bout once a month. I'd guess t'will be verra soon again. Is there something you'll be needin', miss? I could have Tom pick it up for you."

"I was thinking of going along next time," Emily said, daydreaming out the window.

"Oh, miss. 'Tis too far to go all in one day. You'd have to go overnight, and your ma and da would not think it proper for you to go alone wi' Tom. I would not like it much mysel', miss." Kelly Rose giggled as she went to the door. "You just let me know what 'tis you need, miss, an' I'll have Tom get it for you."

As Kelly Rose sailed out the door, Emily thought to herself, "I wonder if I should confide in Tom." What she really wanted was information. It would break Elliot and Norah's hearts if they knew. "Why can't I just let it rest?" she asked herself. The staff at the orphanage had told the Trescowes at the time of her adoption that her birth parents were presumed dead. For some reason, Emily wouldn't or couldn't accept this as the final word. She would like to talk with the staff at the orphanage to see if she could extract more details about her parents from the records. Kelly Rose was right. It would be next to impossible for her to go to Tremorna herself. "I must talk to Tom," she decided. "It's the only way."

# CHAPTER 10

Friday morning brought lots of sunshine and a new customer to Rumford Inn. As Emily was finishing her usual breakfast of tea and toast with marmalade, Tudy burst into the kitchen with news of a weary, "but oh so 'andsome" traveler.

"Where does he come from, Tudy? Did he say?" Emily questioned with much enthusiasm, her curiosity aroused when new faces visited Rumford Inn.

"Says 'e's from Helsted, miss. I thought 'tis strange we've never seen 'im afore, but he says he's moved there only a couple of months ago. Got a position at the bank there, miss. All la-di-da he is. A man for the ladies, I'm thinkin', miss." Tudy pranced around the room with her nose in the air—a rather silly sight as Tudy was a very solidly built lady whose disposition usually matched the roughness of her face and hands.

Emily laughed as Kelly Rose entered and froze in shock upon seeing Tudy's antics.

"Oh, what ye lookin' at, girl!" Tudy scolded, as she quickly resumed her normal role, a hot flush appearing suddenly on her cheeks. "Don't stand there wi' your mouth gawpin' and eyes a-bulgin'. Makes ye look daft, it does."

"Aye, well, which one of us looked daft to you, miss?" Kelly Rose asked, winking at Emily as she began to clear the table.

Emily chose not to answer that. Instead she asked, "Tudy, if he lives in Helsted, why is he staying here?"

Kelly Rose cut in before Tudy could answer. "Well, miss. It seems as there will be more customers afore this day is over. There's to be a meetin' of men representin' each bank in the area this evenin' right here at the inn. Is na that exciting, miss? All those men under our roof. Why, I can 'ardly think on it wi'out faintin'." Kelly Rose swooned as if to faint.

"What is his name?" Emily asked between giggles.

" 'Tis Mr. Ned Draper, miss." Tudy interjected. "I'd be careful round 'im if I was you, miss. He's a looker and those are the worst kind."

"My Tom's a looker, and he's sweet as pie, Tudy," Kelly Rose snorted. "Don't go puttin' your fool ideas in her head. She'll likely make up her own mind anyhow, right miss?"

"You two talk as if you are trying to make a match for me again. The only facts we have are his name and where he lives and works. For all we know, he might be a happily married man," Emily said, hoping this would put an end to this conversation. "Tudy, please tell Mother that I'm going to walk over to the bookshop now, and I will be back before tea."

"Morning, miss. You're up early today." Emily swung around. It was Augie. A few years ago, the Trescowes took him in as he had no family and no place to live. Every day, Augie swabbed the tavern floor and cleaned up around the bar in exchange for his keep. He had a room next to the wine cellar and usually drank, rather than ate, his meals.

"Oh, it's you, Augie! You startled me!" Emily exclaimed. "Yes, I am up early. I have a lot of things to do today. And from the looks of things, so do you."

"Aye, miss. Allus somethin' to do 'ere. 'Ave a good day now," Augie mumbled as he continued his work, grudgingly.

As Emily left through the inn entrance, she almost collided with their new guest. "Morning, miss. Lovely day. Lovely inn, too, don't you think?" he said smiling from ear to ear, taking in Emily's appearance in one sweeping glance.

"Good morning, sir. Yes, it is both a lovely day and a lovely inn. My parents own it. Will you be staying with us this evening?" Emily asked very formally, the trace of a grin on her face as she remembered Tudy's impression of the man.

"I and a couple of my colleagues in the banking business, miss. My name is Ned Draper ... and you are?" he asked as he reached for her hand.

"Emily ... Emily Trescowe," she stuttered as he stooped to kiss her hand. "I really must be going, Mr. Draper. It was very nice to meet you." Emily walked away before he could say more.

Ned Draper stood at the entrance of the inn enjoying the view of Miss Emily from behind. "Philip Polvenon is right. She is a beautiful girl," he mused. "I must make sure that we meet again soon—quite soon."

"You got in pretty late again last night, Alexander!" Philip scowled as he slammed down the morning gazette.

"Not at all, Father. In fact, I came right home after dining with the Spensers," Alex replied as he sat down opposite his father.

"Hmm! Must have been a ten-course dinner! I hope you talked about something constructive at least. But on to another topic, Son. What in God's name ever possessed you to do what you did at the mine yesterday? Do you know how humiliated I was? To think that my son would stoop so low as to run to the aid of a mere bal maiden. It is positively insulting!" Philip boomed, jumping up from his chair as if it could contain him no longer.

Alex was trying very hard to control his temper. "I do not see what I did as wrong, nor do I see why it should concern you in the least, Father."

"Because you are my son and I am grooming you to take over the mines, not to be a simpering nursemaid, damn it!"

Alex was on his feet now. Remaining calm, he said, "There was no one else to help her, Father. If you had hired a doctor specifically for the mine sites as I suggested, I would not have had to do what I did."

"Don't start on that again, Alex. There are perfectly good doctors in the villages nearby if one is needed," Philip replied.

"Are you saying one was not needed yesterday?" Alex questioned.

"It was just a fainting spell, I tell you. Nothing to worry about. She would have come to on her own without your help, Alex," his father grumbled as he stared out the window. "Her own people would have taken her home, and that's as it should be."

Alex sighed audibly. "I know we don't see eye to eye on this, Father. I am trying to learn all there is to know about this mining business, but there is more to it than the business side. Your employees are real people with real problems and real lives; they are just different from ours. They need jobs, yes, but they also need our help and understanding at times. All I'm asking is that you try to see both sides of the picture."

Philip winced as he turned upon his son, looking for a moment as though he would lash out, but thought better of it and said instead, "I will not continue this conversation, Alex. You are going to learn this business in the manner I see fit. Keep your pretty little speeches to yourself, and we'll get along just fine. Now come along; we have work to do."

Alex threw his hands in the air, a look of resignation on his face as he followed his father in silence.

# CHAPTER 11

"Good morning, Hugh!" Emily sang as she swung through the shop door.

"Good morning to you, Miss Emily. 'Tis a fine day, too!" Hugh said as he closed the catalog he had been pouring over for the last hour. "Just browsing today?"

'Actually, I came to see if you have found any information for me about the orphanage," Emily replied, trying not to appear overly anxious.

"Well, there isn't much information, Miss Emily, just that it was built in 1788, and it is the only orphanage in the area. I do have a map showing how to get there. Are you and your parents planning a trip to Tremorna soon?" Hugh asked, hoping he didn't sound too curious.

"Oh, no, Hugh," Emily said, wondering whether she should confide in him any further. "You see, I still have memories of the orphanage and am interested in possibly visiting it again one day soon."

"Well, Miss Emily, 'tis a journey of about two days according to this map. Were you interested in purchasing the map?"

Emily knew that she had made a trip to the shop earlier in the week for the sole purpose of obtaining the map, but now that Tom Stone was going to search out information for her, it was not necessary that she purchase it. However, instead of explaining anything further to Hugh Spenser, she said, "Yes, please, Hugh. And as long as I am here, I'd like to browse a bit."

"Certainly, Miss Emily," Hugh smiled. "Why t'wouldn't be the same if you didn't, now would it?"

Emily grinned at Hugh as she walked down the aisle to the novel section. "Hugh is such a nice man," she thought, as she browsed through the eye level shelf first. Emily had decided long ago that she was very fortunate to live in the only town for miles around that had its own bookshop. She loved to read. It was her passion. She would sit for hours on the stone bench behind Rumford Inn or go to the docks and sit with her feet in the water and read and read. She lost herself in the stories she read and would many times be late for meals or chores because of it.

As she was paging through a book entitled *Tessa*, she heard the door of the shop open and close. She looked up and saw Alex Polvenon smiling at her from the other end of the aisle. As he walked slowly toward her, her heart skipped a beat. It had been over a week since he had come to her rescue. Whatever would she say to him? She felt tongue-tied.

"We meet again, Miss Emily," Alex said as he bowed to her. "You are looking very well. I trust you have fully recuperated from your rather bumpy ride home the other day. Did you find your family and friends in good health?"

"Y-yes, I did, Mr. Polvenon. Th-thank you again for rescuing me. I don't know what I would possibly have done without your help," Emily replied, wondering if she sounded as nervous as she felt.

"As I've said before, Miss Emily, it was no trouble at all, and as I had the pleasure of your company, the ride back to Polvenon Cove was a most delightful one."

"Those eyes," thought Emily. "They are gorgeous. But I wish he wouldn't look at me like that."

"Well, nonetheless, thank you again. It was very much appreciated, Mr. Polvenon," Emily said as calmly as she could.

"Oh, please, Miss Emily, after sharing an enchanting afternoon together, surely you can call me Alex. I would feel most honored if you would consider me a friend." Before she could respond, he continued, "I see that you enjoy novels. I too have a passion for reading."

"Oh?" questioned Emily. "In what type of books do your interests lie, Mr....Alex?" Alex beamed a smile at Emily that would have made any woman melt. "I must be careful," thought Emily, "or I will surely fall under his spell."

"I love reading about other lands. I can close my eyes and imagine I am there. Not that I don't love it right where I am," he said as he took in her shy smile and her beautiful blush. "Have you ever longed to live somewhere else, Miss Emily?"

"No," Emily replied emphatically. "I love it here. I can't believe that any other place would be lovelier than Cornwall. There is such a beauty in this rugged coastline. I especially love it when the wind blows the waves up over the cliffs, and the villages seem so clean and fresh after a good storm."

"Well, well, I see we have something else in common, Miss Emily!" Alex cried. "I, too, love the smell of the sea air after a storm has passed through. Have you ever walked out on the cliffs just after the rain?"

"Yes, many times, and it is truly breathtaking," Emily replied, wondering what it would be like to walk along the footpath with Alex at her side.

As if reading her thoughts, Alex said, "Then that is something I hope that I may look forward to in the near future—a walk with you after the very next rain."

"Oh, Alex, I don't think ..." But before Emily could finish her sentence, Hugh's voice came out of nowhere.

"Hello, Alex. I didn't even see you there. I heard someone come in but didn't know it was you. Are you helping Miss Emily with her selection or interrupting her browsing?" Hugh said laughingly as he slapped Alex on the back and gave him a wink.

"Actually, Hugh, not that it is any business of yours," Alex teased, "Miss Emily and I are fast becoming friends. I am finding her taste in books and weather fascinating."

Hugh looked puzzled as he threw a questioning glance at Emily. "Hugh, Mr. Pol ... Alex and I have met before. You see, he came to my—"

"I'm sorry to interrupt, Miss Emily," Hugh laughed, "but Alex has already told us the story of your dilemma and how he rescued you. Although, as he relates it, it seems as though you rescued him from a rather boring business meeting that day."

Emily smiled at Alex as she put the book back on the shelf. "Well, this has been very nice, but I really must be going. I will, indeed, purchase the map, Hugh." She turned to Alex. "It was nice seeing you again, Alex." She took the coins from her purse to purchase the map and said goodbye. Alex followed her through the shop door and out into the sunny street.

"May I walk you home, Miss Emily?"

"Oh, that won't be necessary, Alex. I am sure you have something more important to tend to," Emily replied as she started to walk away.

"I hope I will have the pleasure of seeing you again very soon, Miss Emily!" Alex shouted after Emily who had picked up her pace, glad of the encounter, but eager to get home and tell Kelly Rose all about it.

# CHAPTER 12

Later that same day, Emily was out in front of Rumford Inn picking flowers to place on the tables for that evening's meeting of bankers. She thought of how pleasant Mr. Draper had been earlier and laughed as she pictured Tudy dancing around the kitchen, mimicking the way he walked. But Tudy was right. There was something about Mr. Ned Draper that seemed a little dangerous, and she promised herself not to engage in any flirtatious behavior around him.

Emily looked up at the sound of the familiar creaks and clinks of Mr. Terwilliger's cart as he came around the corner and halted at the inn. " 'Ullo to ye, Miss Emily!" he shouted as he leaped from his perch and landed clumsily at her feet. "Now is na that just like ye to pick flowers for me just as I be comin' down the lane." He winked as he bowed and kissed her hand.

"You are right again, Mr. Terwilliger," Emily teased, tucking a bright yellow mum into the brim of his hat. "Actually, we are getting ready for a meeting of bankers here at the inn tonight."

"Oh, aye. I've seen 'em on the road. Few of 'em are 'headin' this way as we speak."

"Mr. Terwilliger," Emily said curiously, "have you ever heard of a Mr. Ned Draper?"

"Who hasn't, miss?" he chuckled, a sly grin on his face. " 'E's got a bit of the devil in 'im, that one does. Likes the ladies and the ladies likes 'im. Met 'im, have ye, miss?"

"Yes, this morning. I was about to walk to the bookshop when our paths crossed. He seems nice enough. A little too sure of himself, though, I think."

"Aye, men like 'im always are sure of themselves. Turned your 'ead a bit, has 'e? Be careful, Miss Emily. Thems the kind to watch out for. Well, I be plenty thirsty, miss, so I'll be on my way inside now," Mr. Terwilliger said, already shuffling toward the inn.

As Emily finished her task, she pondered Tudy and Mr. Terwilliger's warnings about Ned Draper. Was he dangerous? Or was he just mysterious? He was so pleasant and seemed very interested in seeing her again. She pictured his light, wavy hair and his blue-grey eyes. He certainly was handsome. Not in the same way as Alexander Polvenon. Just the opposite, really, but handsome just the same. It wouldn't hurt to speak with him again and find out more about him. Already, she had forgotten her promise to herself that she would be cautious where Ned Draper was concerned.

Emily found Tom taking inventory in the storeroom at the back of the inn. "Good morning, Tom."

Tom nearly jumped out of his skin. "Well, good morning to you, lass. You gave me quite a scare. It is na every day I get visitors back here, leastways not such pretty ones." He smiled as he set his list down on a table. "What can I do for you, lass?" he asked.

"Kelly Rose told me that you'd be going into Tremorna soon, Tom," Emily said.

"Oh, aye, lass. On the morrow, to be exact. And what would you be needin' from there, eh?" Tom asked, surprised at her interest in his pending trip.

"Tom," Emily whispered, signaling him to come closer, "can you keep a secret?"

"Me?" Tom asked with amused suspicion. "Oh, aye. You can trust me to keep me mouth shut, that you can, lass."

"I just need it to be kept from my mother and father as I don't want to hurt or upset them, Tom. But I need to know if there is any more information you could get about my birth parents from the orphanage in Tremorna. All anyone's been told is that they are dead or presumed dead. What I would like to know, Tom, is if they did die, how did it happen? That must be in the records, don't you think?" Emily asked, looking anxiously at Tom.

"Ah, well now, lass," Tom said quietly. "I don't know as I'd get any more information than you already know, but it wouldn't hurt to try, would it now? You just leave it to ol' Tom here. If there's anything to be found out, I'll find it, lass, don't you worry. He gave her long chestnut locks a little tug. Emily was so relieved; she hugged him tightly.

"Thank you so much, Tom. This means a lot to me. I'll repay you somehow."

"No need for that, lass. You make me smile and that's enough for me. Now off wi' you. I've work to do." He shooed her out of the room with an imaginary broom. She giggled as she ran out. Tom watched her as she disappeared around the corner. He immediately lost his smile as he thought about Emily's obsession with her real parents. "I wish she would let it lay, aye, I do. No good will come of it," Tom thought to himself as he turned to finish the inventory.

Tom Stone departed for Tremorna the next morning, kissing Kelly Rose soundly and waving to Emily, who was up early to see him off, something she did not normally do. Tom looked a bit anxious as he jumped up on the wagon and left them behind. He was still troubled about Emily's request to find out what he could about her birth parents. Hadn't Elliot and Norah Trescowe provided Emily with a stable, happy, loving home? Why wasn't that enough for Emily? He pondered the situation as he plodded along. His father had known a girl years ago who had conceived out of wedlock and had been banished from the village. As far as his father knew, that girl had had her child and had left it on the orphanage doorstep. Was Emily this child? How could her mother just leave her like that? Where was the mother now? These were questions that had bothered Tom ever since he began working for the Trescowes. He had never divulged his suspicions to anyone. Tom hoped with all his heart that his visit to Tremorna Orphanage would turn up no new information. If it did, should he keep it from Emily? She was determined to find out about her birth parents, no matter what it took.

Tom was always in awe when he passed Polvenon Manor. It was so majestic and yet tragic. It was once a beautiful estate with luscious lawns and carefully tended gardens. Now, even though the manor still stood in all its glory, the grounds were a shamble.

As Tom passed by on his way to Tremorna, he noticed some movement behind the manor house. As he watched closely, he saw that it was the servant, Benjamin, and he was walking briskly and determinedly toward the wooded area at the back of the estate carrying a basket. "Strange place to have a picnic," Tom mused. "Those woods haven't been cleared since Lord knows when." With a shrug of his shoulders and a chuckle, Tom continued on his journey.

Alex had come home midday to get a change of clothing, as he was filthy from doing the inventory in the stockroom. It was rare for either of the Polvenon men to come home at that time of the day. As Alex went into the kitchen to fix a sandwich for himself, Benjamin was just shuffling in the back door of the kitchen with a basketful of what looked like bed linens and towels.

"What's this?" Alex exclaimed as Benjamin dropped the basket with a thud onto the floor, a look of horror on his face.

"Oh, M-Master Alex! You startled me! I w-was airing these things out back and was just b-bringing them inside." Benjamin seemed surprised by his own clever ruse. Just as he was beginning to think that his explanation was sufficient, Alex proceeded to rummage through the contents of the basket. "Benjamin, my good man. Why, these linens have holes in them the size of my hand. I pity the poor soul who must sleep with these on his bed. Certainly, you are not using these on any of the beds in this house, are you?" Alex asked, puzzled as to why these linens had not yet been made into rags.

A tense little giggle escaped Benjamin's lips. "Of course not, Master Alex. Not in this house, I mean, I was only airing them so I could pack them up and ship them off to the poor house," he stammered as he grabbed the basket and hurried from the room before Alex could ask any more questions.

# CHAPTER 13

Emily lay in bed later than usual the morning after the bankers' meeting. It had seemed as though Mr. Draper eyed her every time she walked into the room to refill the water jugs. During a break in the meeting, he had tried to search her out but was unsuccessful as she kept to her room most of the evening. She had told Kelly Rose about her exciting meeting with Alex Polvenon at the bookshop. Kelly Rose had warned her about going out walking with Mr. Polvenon alone so soon after making his acquaintance. Emily knew Kelly Rose was right, but it's what she wanted most in the world—to be alone with Alex Polvenon. She closed her eyes again and pictured her and Alex walking along the clifftops, hand in hand, looking out at the beauty of the sparkling sea and the rugged coastline.

A light rap on the door brought her back to the present. "Come in," she said softly.

"Good morning, dear," Norah sang as she walked into the room, looking at Emily, her heart skipping a beat as it so often did when Emily did or said something that triggered a memory of her own dear sister. At times, it seemed uncanny, Norah mused, as she opened the brightly colored chintz curtains. "Are you feeling all right? It's not like you to stay in bed so long."

"Oh, I'm fine, Mother." Emily yawned as she hopped out of bed. "Do you think Tudy left me any crumbs for breakfast?" she teased as she splashed cold water on her face.

"I think she can muster something up for you, dear," Norah laughed as she helped her to make her bed. "Emily, how would you like to visit Joanna today? I thought I'd pack a basket and go with you. I haven't seen Joanna's mother in a very long while, and I think now would be a good time. I would like to see if there is anything I can do to help. She must have her hands full, what with Joanna being ill and the little ones to look after."

"That would be nice. The other day when I visited Joanna, she was still very ill. I hope that she is doing better." Emily had her doubts, however. She did not want to upset Norah unduly, but she did seem to be getting worse.

After a quick breakfast of toast and marmalade with tea, Emily and Norah set out for the Simmons home in Helsted.

After finishing his business in Tremorna, Tom went to visit the orphanage. It was a drizzly autumn afternoon, but Tom was immune to the fine Cornish mist. He loved the untamed coast, the contorted, wind-bent coppers and birches, the open moors and steep-sided valleys. As he was passing the magnificent Holly Bay and its estuary, he could see Tremorna Orphanage just ahead.

It was a tearful Mrs. Simmons who answered Norah's knock. "Oh, Mrs. Trescowe! How good of you to come! Oh, but I'm afeared, I am. 'Tis bad. Our Joanna is—mortal bad." she said as she wept into her apron.

Norah quickly placed her basket on the table and ran to comfort Mrs. Simmons. "Oh, my dear, I am so sorry. Has the doctor been to see her?" she asked as she rocked the poor woman in her arms.

Mrs. Simmons began to sob even harder. "Oh, aye, Mrs. Trescowe. 'E be called just this mornin," she said quietly, her head bent as if in shame. "I blame meself, for 'tis I who held off fetchin' 'im. Thought she'd lose 'er place at the mine if the master knew. No place for ill ones there, ye know. First sign of the sickness they gets rid of 'em, they do. Won't make it wi' just the little one's wages. Don't see 'ow, Mrs. Trescowe. Oh, 'taint 'bout me I'm worrit; I can get along jus' fine. 'Tis my babies I gotta think of. I'd give all I got to see my Joanna healthy and on her feet again. Oh, what am I to do; whatever am I to do?" she cried as she wiped her eyes on the kerchief Norah handed to her.

Emily ached for the Simmons woman. However, she was very anxious about Joanna and decided to slip into her room while Norah consoled Mrs. Simmons so she could see her friend alone for a few minutes.

Emily was not prepared for the sight that met her eyes as she entered Joanna's room and tiptoed to the edge of her bed. Surely this was not her best friend. Joanna had always had a pale, rather pallid complexion, but this was truly a ghost. Emily quickly bit her lower lip to hold back a sob as she realized how close to death Joanna was. She gently laid her hand over Joanna's, tears running freely. "Oh, Joanna. Is there nothing that can be done? Why did this have to happen to you?" Emily slouched onto the bed and laid her head on Joanna's chest, gathering her into her arms as best she could, wailing uncontrollably now. Why did Joanna and her family have such a hard life? Why did some people have nothing while others had too much? "It isn't fair!" Emily cried aloud, suddenly shocked out of her lamenting by a slight touch on her head. Emily sprang up, hope and fear mingled in her eyes as she realized that Joanna had moved. "Joanna," Emily gasped. "Can you hear me? It's Emily."

Joanna's eyes flickered as she tried to focus on her good friend. Yes, she had heard Emily sobbing and wanted to console her—tell her that dying was not a bad thing after all. She wanted to tell her that she felt more at peace at this moment than at any time in her short life. Any fears she had left were for her family and their future. She gathered all the strength she could and spoke so softly to Emily that Emily had to place her ear very near Joanna's mouth to catch all that she was saying.

"Emily, my dear, dear friend. Do no' cry for me. I'm goin' to a peaceful place where there is na any worrin' to do nor bein' hungry anymore. Be 'appy for me, Emily." Joanna had to stop as she felt another cough coming on. Emily gave her a sip of water, and after a few moments Joanna resumed. "Emily, I want to tell ye somethin'. One of the happiest days of my life was the day Master Alex swept me up on his horse an' rode me home. It were like a dream. But 'twas not for that I were happiest— 'twas because 'e asked about ye, Emily—asked everything 'e could in that short a time, 'e did. I knew then that 'e felt somethin' special like for ye, my best friend. It made me so happy! Be good to 'im, Emily. A nice man, 'e is. Nicer than most. I want everthin' that's best for ye. I love ye, Emily Trescowe." Joanna smiled and sighed softly as she closed her eyes. As her hand slid from Emily's, Emily clutched it and held it to her lips, saying goodbye as she kissed it. "I love you too, Joanna Simmons, and I'll do all I can to make sure that your family is taken care of. Oh, I'll miss you so!"

Emily sat there for a long time. She did not think. She was numb.

To his relief, Tom came away from the orphanage with no new information about Emily's real parents. Sister Therese, who was in charge of records, checked through the files and found that Emily was indeed left on the doorstep of the orphanage shortly after her birth. She had remained living in the orphanage until she was four years old at which time the Trescowes adopted her. Tom asked Sister Therese if she or anyone else at the orphanage had ever known of any young women living in Tremorna at that time who may have been the mother or who may have suddenly disappeared. Sister Therese said that there was a search for the mother, but as far as they could tell, the mother was not from Tremorna and that both parents were presumed dead.

Tom thanked Sister Therese and left a small donation, which Emily had given him from her savings. He could go back to Emily and tell her, in good conscience, that he found nothing new to report. He was glad. Maybe this would put her mind at ease once and for all.

Tom looked forward to his next stop. Tremorna had the only jeweler in the area. He had had his eye on an engagement ring and had been scrimping and saving every tip he received from the customers at Rumford Inn in anticipation of purchasing that ring to place on Kelly Rose's finger. He loved her so much. He was certain she loved him. And now, at least, he had enough money to buy it for her. He came out of the jeweler's shop, his face beaming as brightly as the ring in the box in his pocket. It would take him almost two days to get back to Polvenon Cove, but to Tom, it seemed it would take weeks.

# CHAPTER 14

Norah and Emily were silent companions on the way home from Helsted. A storm was brewing and the wind was so loud, it made conversation almost impossible. Heads bowed and caps knotted up tight against the weather, they nearly ran the last half of the way home as the skies opened up and unleashed a torrent of rain and hail.

Once safe, warm, and dry inside the inn, Norah set about her late afternoon duties with fervor attempting to block out the pain and loss she had seen on the little faces of the Simmons children and the guilt and anguish that seemed to leave an indelible mark on Joanna's mother. She could certainly sympathize with them, having lost her sister Margaret years ago—the suffering and worrying of not knowing if she was dead or alive—her body never found, nor that of her lover, Drake Monroe. The only comfort for the Simmons family was in knowing that their beautiful Joanna had passed into a better life and that after a period of mourning, they could try to put back the pieces of their lives and move on. Norah sighed, dabbing at her eyes as she scrubbed the vegetables for their evening meal.

Emily's sorrow, on the other hand, took the form a blind anger. Alone in her room, she screamed into her pillow, pounded her fists into the mattress and, in desperation, threw her beloved teddy bear against the wall. "Why, why, oh why!" she shrieked, then finally broke into a fit of sobbing which lasted a good half hour.

Eyes burning and head pounding, Emily sat up silently. The storm had abated, and the sun was peeking through as if to say a quick hello before setting. Emily grabbed a dry cloak and quietly stole down the back stairs and out into the cool, crisp, clean air. She began to walk with no destination in mind. She just needed to walk. She needed to understand why Joanna had to die. She didn't know where to begin. "How do I find the answer?" she asked herself over and over again as she began the slow incline toward the cliff path. She walked so far that she didn't even see that she had passed Polvenon Manor and was halfway to Helsted.

Moments later she found herself sitting on one of the benches near the path—put there as a rest stop for weary hikers or for people, like herself, who would come up here with a good book or to think or admire the view. "It is so peaceful up here." Emily sighed. "Oh, Joanna, I do hope heaven is just like this."

Not realizing that she spoke aloud, Emily jumped as a voice came from behind her. "You took the words right out of my mouth."

She swung around with a startled, "Oh! I didn't know you were here." She started to get up as Alex Polvenon walked up to her.

"Please, sit down. I didn't mean to interrupt your thoughts," Alex said as Emily hesitantly sat down again. At any other time, Emily would have been flustered to have Alex find her like this—eyes red and swollen, tears still drying on her face. But today she didn't care.

"Actually, Mr. Pol ... Alex," she said, "I'm glad you interrupted my thoughts. They are not happy ones, I'm afraid." Emily quickly looked down as her eyes began to fill.

Alex noticed her distress and quietly asked, "Are you all right, Miss Emily?"

"No, I am not all right. Something is wrong. Terribly wrong! Joanna Simmons died today, and it shouldn't have happened, Alex. It just shouldn't have." Emily paused for a second, looked straight into Alex's deep blue eyes and stated simply, "And if I am to call you Alex, you are to call me Emily—just Emily." Once again, she began to weep bitterly. Within seconds, Emily was wrapped in the arms of Alex, words of comfort pouring out from his heart to hers, easing her troubled mind back into some sense of saneness.

"Oh, Emily. I am so sorry. You are right; it should never have happened. She was so young." Emily could feel his body tense as he tried to control the sudden onslaught of emotions—the anger and hatred toward his father for the poor working conditions at the mine, the sorrow he felt for Joanna and her family, but also the happiness and rightness of holding Emily close as he comforted her.

As time passed, Emily became still. She felt a sort of peace being here with Alex. "Thank you, Alex," she whispered as she looked up into his face and saw compassion and something else she couldn't quite put her finger on.

He smiled softly down at her, kissed her forehead and said, "Come, Emily. Let me take you home. It's getting dark and the wind is picking up again." He took her by the hand and helped her from the bench. As they began to walk, it started to pour again, this time so hard and heavy that they were both drenched as they neared Polvenon Manor.

"Emily, you must come to my home and dry off by the fireplace. You will likely catch pneumonia if we continue walking like this. While you warm yourself, I will get Benjamin to ready the carriage, and I will take you home."

"Oh, I couldn't possibly." Emily stammered, shivering as she wondered what to do. Common sense told her to go with him, but proper etiquette told her to go straight home. Common sense won out as Alex insisted, leading her by the arm up the many granite steps to the front door of the manor, which Emily had always considered rather ominous. The inside of the estate was just as awe-inspiring. The dark paneled front hall, lit only by candles in heavy iron wall sconces, was larger than all of Rumford Inn. A massive staircase opposite the front entrance was covered with once beautiful but now threadbare Turkish carpeting. Portraits lined the wall leading up the stairs, but it was too dark to see any of them from where Emily stood.

"This way, Emily." Alex led her to a room to the left of the staircase. As soon as he opened the door, she felt warmth, not only from the roaring fire someone had already started in the fireplace but also from the décor. "This is my father's study, and it's also the warmest room in the house. We sit in here most evenings, that is, for as long as we can stand each other." Alex chuckled softly to himself as he directed her to a chair near the fireplace. "If you will pardon me for a few minutes, Emily, I will go and tell Benjamin to ready the carriage." Emily nodded toward Alex, shivering despite the warmth, which seemed to be already drying her garments.

As Alex left the room, she took her cloak and spread it on the floor near the fireplace. "So this is Polvenon Manor," she mused. As she scanned the room with her eyes, she noticed that the character of it denoted a woman's touch at one time. Faded crimson paper dotted with pale roses covered those walls not lined with bookshelves. Deep red velvet draperies were already drawn shut for the evening. A large rug of the same hue edged with a geometric design intertwined with once-pink roses covered most of the hardwood floor. Manly paraphernalia lined the mantle except for a small silver trinket box, intricately etched with a tiny floral pattern. Above the mantle hung the portrait of a most beautiful woman. "This must be Alex's mother!" Emily exclaimed aloud.

"Who are you? And what are you doing in my study?" boomed a voice from the entryway. Emily swung around, stumbling over her words in an effort to explain. At that instant, Alex came into the room and began to introduce Emily to his father but stopped midway, startled by the look on his father's face as he stared openly at Emily. The color had visibly drained from his face. He took a few steps backward, grasping the arm of a chair to keep his balance.

"Father, are you all right?" Alex cried as he ran to steady him. "You look as though you've seen a ghost. What is it, Father?"

Philip looked distraught. Emily was at a loss for words. Obviously, her presence had unnerved the man. As Alex attempted to calm his father, Emily, confused and anxious, grabbed her cloak from the floor and ran from the room. Alex called after her, but to no avail. As Emily reached the front entrance and opened the door to depart, a manservant quickly jumped aside to avoid a collision with her. A shocked gasp emitted from his lips as he clasped his hands to his mouth in an effort to stifle it. "The carriage is ready, miss," he said breathlessly as he continued to stare wide-eyed.

"No, thank you! I will walk home." Tears blinding her, she nearly fell down the steps in her struggle to get away. The rain had let up a little, but she still ran most of the way home. It was dark and late, and Norah and Elliot would certainly be worried. "Oh, what an awful day!" Emily cried as she finally reached the warming glow coming from Rumford Inn.

# CHAPTER 15

The sun broke through the clouds bright and early the next morning. Alex puzzled over the events of last evening as he dressed. With the help of Benjamin, they got his father to his room and tucked in for the night. Alex had never seen his father like that before. "What brought it on?" he wondered. After poor Emily had taken leave of the house, Philip had not said another word. He just sat and stared at the spot where Emily had been standing. It was so unlike his father. He was always full of things to say, usually contrary. The tone Phillip used when he first spoke to Emily was what Alex would have expected. However, when Emily turned to face him, Philip's reaction rendered him almost helpless. Was it her voice as she tried to explain her reason for being there? Was it her beauty that stunned his father into speechlessness?

Whatever it was, it frightened Alex. To the outside world, Philip Polvenon was a terrible man. He was a wicked old miser who used others for his own gain. Alex knew the truth of this all too well. He also knew the reason.

Alex grew up without a mother. Alexa Aitherton was deeply in love with Philip and he with her. Before Philip met Alexa, his life had been a happy one. Meeting and later marrying Alexa made his life even more ideal. They lived at Polvenon Manor with his parents, Edward and Caroline. Eleven months after their wedding, Alexa died giving birth to their son, Alexander. She was twenty-two years old. The light had gone out of Philip's life. But he had his son and his servant, Benjamin. Benjamin had been living at Polvenon Manor since birth. His mother had been Philip's nanny. Philip and Benjamin grew up together and became very close, even though Benjamin had eventually been groomed to become Philip's manservant.

Shortly after Alexa's death, Philip had met and fallen in love with a beautiful woman, a woman who did not return his love. Philip was shattered. It was this rejection and loneliness that, over the years, had transformed Philip Polvenon into a tortured, bitter soul.

"What are you doing up at this god-awful hour?" Alex jumped at this remark, unaware that his father had entered the room. "Don't just stand there; tell Benjamin to bring my breakfast!" Alex stood still for a minute longer, noticing as he gazed at his father that he looked shaken still. He seemed unable to look at Alex but fumbled about, rifling through papers, finally walking, a bit unsteadily, over to the window.

Perplexed and confused, Alex slowly questioned his father. "Father, breakfast can wait. What happened last night to put you in such a state?"

Philip coughed nervously and mumbled as he continued to stare out the window. "You are making much out of nothing. I was merely startled to find someone standing in my study, someone, mind you, I had not invited."

"But I invited her, Father," Alex interrupted defensively.

"I hope that you are not going to tell me that this female is a friend of yours, Alexander. And just what was she doing in my study anyway?" Philip boomed loud enough for Benjamin to hear in the kitchen.

"She is becoming a very dear ..."

"No!" Philip roared. "I will not have it! Stay away from her, do you hear me, Alex? If you know what is good for you, you will never see her again! And I forbid her in this house!"

"This is my house, too, Father, and you cannot dictate who my friends will be!" Alex shouted back at his father, at this moment anger overcoming respect. "What has come over you? Tell me what happened last night to upset you. I don't understand."

Philip whipped around to stare at his son. Alex could see his father trying to gain control of his temper. Philip took one deep, calming breath and, in a bone-chilling monotone, stated, "Women are evil, Son. Stay away from her." He quietly left the room, evidently forgetting about his breakfast.

Alex paced as he puzzled aloud over his father's behavior. "His blanket statement that 'women are evil' surely did not include Emily. If only he would give her a chance, get to know her, he would certainly come to love her as I do." Startled, Alex plopped into the nearest chair in open-mouthed amazement. He realized what he had just said. He loved Emily. That girl had stolen into his life and captured his heart. So innocent and complete was his love for her that it filled him with awe. Unbeknownst to him, a smile had spread across his face, and as he rose from the chair, he practically flew into the kitchen. Suddenly, he was starving. He would deal with his father later.

Benjamin was tiptoeing through the back door with a basket under his arm as Alex bolted into the kitchen. "What's in the basket, Benjamin? Don't tell me you were out on a picnic already this morning," Alex teased.

"Ah, that is funny, Master Alex! Yes, yes, very funny." Benjamin giggled nervously as Alex rummaged through the larder.

"Where's last evening's bread, Benjamin? I want some with preserves this morning."

Quickly stowing the basket out of sight in hopes that it wouldn't trigger any more questions, Benjamin said, "Well, Master Alex, I have just baked some apple muffins—your favorite."

"Hmm. Very tempting, Benjamin, but what I really want is some of that bread. I believe it was quite the best I've ever tasted."

"Well ..."

Alex turned to Benjamin, looking him straight in the eyes. "All right Benjamin. I want to know what you've been up to lately."

"I don't know what you mean, Master Alex. Benjamin said so quietly with head bent so that Alex had to lean forward to hear him.

"What I mean, Benjamin, is that this isn't the first time food, not to mention other items from this household, have gone missing. This also isn't the first time I've seen you sneak in or out the back door carrying either a basket, tray, or some other such bundle. Up until now, you have not given me a reason for this behavior that satisfies me. I want the truth, Benjamin, now!"

Benjamin jumped at the growing irritation in Alex's voice. With a sigh of resignation, he began, "Master Alex, there is a poor family down in the village whom I have taken it upon myself to aid. I have not mentioned it to Master Philip because, well ..."

"Yes, I know why, Benjamin." Alex sighed. "Go on."

"I have taken only food that was left over and some rather old linens that would have been used as rags, things that would be of no use to either you or your father," Benjamin explained.

"Well, I could have used some of that bread this morning," Alex said rather testily, but when Benjamin turned to look at him, he winked as he grabbed two apple muffins and began spreading them with jam. "A family, you say? Is there a father, Benjamin? Does he work in the mines?"

"Well, no, Master Alex. No father."

"Well, I approve wholeheartedly, Benjamin. Don't worry; your secret will stay between us. I'll take tea in the other room, by the way." Just before leaving the kitchen, Alex turned and teased, "Just don't go sweet on the woman, Benjamin. You know how Father would feel about that."

Benjamin let out a sigh of relief as he stumbled into the nearest chair. "That was too close," he thought. He'd have to be much more careful from now on. He couldn't let an incident like this happen again. He couldn't be found out. It would cost him his job and much more— oh so much more!

# CHAPTER 16

Emily's thoughts raced back and forth between the death of her best friend and the very puzzling incident at Polvenon Manor the night before. Poor Joanna. There is such a risk of disease for those who are born into that way of life. Even as a bal maiden, working on the dressing floor, the air was surely not as deadly as down in the mines, but all the dust from crushing those rocks day in and day out—no fit job for a woman much less a child. The conditions in which the Simmons family had had to live since the death of their father certainly had much to do with the very swift deterioration of Joanna's health. Except for Mrs. Simmons, all the children were very thin. Worn garments hung limply on their little bodies. The rooms in the cottage were not heated, except for a constant, but small fire going in the kitchen, and each time Emily stopped for a visit, there seemed not to be enough food to go around. Tears rolled down Emily's face as she wondered how the family was going to survive and how she was going to go on without one of her very best friends in the world.

Emily's sorrow soon turned to anger when she remembered that the Simmons family was not unlike many families who worked the mines. The poor working conditions could be much improved if only the mine owners would care enough to invest in better equipment and machinery. Increasing the wages of the men so that their women and children would not have to work would be an idea very foreign to Philip Polvenon.

"Miss Emily. Are ye awake? May I come in then?

"Oh, yes, Kelly Rose." Emily jumped as Kelly Rose flew into her room.

"Are ye all right, miss? We were all gettin' worrit. 'Tis late, it is. Breakfast is waitin'. We all happen to know that ye were a wee bit late gettin' in last night." Kelly Rose glanced sideways at Emily, eyebrows arched in a question.

"I'll tell you all about it later, Kelly Rose. Last evening was very puzzling and strange—rather frightening. It will probably all come out at breakfast as they will want to know where I was. If they are waiting, we'd best go down now."

Kelly rose stopped Emily with a gentle hug. "Oh, Miss Emily, before we go, let me say how sorry I am about your friend. 'Tis sad for you and her family, but she be at peace now and 'tis best for her."

Emily hugged Kelly Rose tightly, trying to pull herself together. "Thank you, Kelly Rose. You, too, are a dear friend, and I don't know what I'd do without you."

Emily wasn't very hungry this morning. Tudy had prepared eggs, rashers, and toast, but Emily only ate a piece of dry toast and sipped some tea. Norah and Elliot could see the pain in Emily's eyes and did not pressure her as to where she was the night before. They were shocked, therefore, when Emily, looking down at her plate, said, "I was at Polvenon Manor last night." Elliot cleared his throat and glanced over at Norah, who was staring at Emily in astonishment.

"Polvenon Manor? But, whatever possessed you to go there of all places? I don't understand, Emily," Elliot queried. Norah looked relieved that he had taken it upon himself to question Emily.

"Actually, it was because of the rain, Father. You see, after we came home from Helsted, the rain had let up a bit, and I felt as though I needed to walk to get out in the fresh air and think. I had walked quite a distance along the cliff path when a voice startled me. It was Alex Polvenon. Do you remember the day I came home from school? I did not tell you because I didn't want to upset you, but the carriage I was traveling in broke down quite a way from here—too far to carry my bags. Well, another carriage, the Polvenon family carriage, came to my rescue and took me home. That is when I met Alexander Polvenon." Emily had a faraway look in her eyes. Norah and Elliot raised their eyebrows in unison.

"And that gives Mr. Polvenon the right to follow you along the cliff path?" Elliot asked, a firmness in his voice that wasn't there before.

"Oh no, Father. It wasn't that way at all! You see, we had met again since the carriage ride. I saw him at the bookstore the other day, and he was kind enough to walk part of the way home with me. He is such a nice man."

"Yes, yes," Elliot interjected, disbelief in his tone. "I have never met the man, but if he is anything like his father ..."

"That is what is so strange. He is nothing like his father. They are different as night and day, at least from what I could gather last night."

If Elliot's interest hadn't peaked before, it did now. "Last night! You mean you met his father last night?"

"Well, not exactly. You see, Alex walked with me back down the path, and it started to rain buckets. We were getting soaked through and, as we were closer to Polvenon Manor than Rumford Inn, he suggested that we dry ourselves by the fire and then he would take me home in the carriage." At this Norah stiffened in her chair, but remained silent. Emily noticed this. She also saw the tight-lipped expression on Elliot's face. "I know what this must sound like, but it truly was raining hard, and the wind wasn't helping. I felt I had no choice."

At that moment, Kelly Rose, who had been in and out of the dining room during breakfast, chimed in. " 'Tis not that I was listening in on purpose like. But I also happen to know t'was pouring buckets last night, because Tom and I were out in it too. Leave it to Tom to pick the most blustery, devilish night there was to propose to me."

"What? He finally did it? Oh, Kelly Rose, that's wonderful!" Emily jumped up and gave her a big hug, happy for her and relieved that the subject had been changed, at least for now. "Where's Tom? I must congratulate him!"

"He'll be in the wine cellar about now, Miss Emily!" Kelly Rose shouted as Emily was already out the kitchen door. Norah and Elliot both wished Kelly Rose all the best and asked if they had made any plans yet.

"All we do know, Miss Norah, Master Elliot, is that you are like family and if 'tis all right, we'd like to stay on right here." The Trescowes told Kelly Rose they couldn't be happier for her and Tom and that they were very relieved to know that they would remain at Rumford Inn.

# CHAPTER 17

Still puzzling over his father's behavior last night, Alexander knew he had to find a way to see Emily. He needed to make sure she got home safely and apologize for his father's strange actions toward her. He had no answers, so how could he explain it to Emily?

"Alex, we must go over these documents today! No more dawdling around." Philip entered the room, waving papers around, looking just as angry as he did last night. Alex knew it would do no good to try to discuss last evening's tirade again and so said, "All right, Father" as he walked over to Philip's desk to study the papers.

"Wait a minute, Father. What's this all about?! You are no longer going to give any type of aid, financial or otherwise, to the minors who are injured on the job?" Now Alex was seeing red! "You can't do this!"

"I can and I am! I am giving them good wages for a good day's work, and that should be enough. It's not my fault if they are careless and hurt themselves. If everyone would just follow the damn rules, there would be no injuries. I refuse to continue to mollycoddle every man, woman, or child who feels it is their right to claim compensation for medical costs. Next they'll expect food and clothing be provided and rent paid.

This is going to stop, and it's going to stop now. I want you to sign these papers and get them over to our solicitor this morning."

Alex looked down at the documents. He shook his head and said, "I cannot sign these, Father. Injuries can happen through no fault of their own, and you know it. You've gone too far this time." Alex threw the papers on the desk and walked out of the room.

Fuming, Philip shouted, "Benjamin! Get in here!"

Benjamin came running, raising his eyebrows when he saw the mess on Philip's desk. "Yes, sir?"

"Take these papers to the solicitor, and do it fast!" Philip straightened the papers and shoved them at Benjamin. "Tell him I want a statement drawn up regarding the contents, and I want him to send it to all our employees immediately, if not sooner."

Hugh was busy checking inventory and his father, Creighton, was in the back room going over the accounts when Alex stormed into the bookshop. "Whoa, there! What's got you all in a tither?" Hugh asked as he pushed his paperwork aside to give Alex his full attention.

"My father! He was so rude to Emily last night that she ran home in the rain." Creighton came to the front when he heard Alex's voice. Alex told them all about the events of the evening before.

Creighton sighed. "He is such a bitter old fool. He never got over losing his wife and then being turned away by that other woman. However, that is no excuse for the way he treated Emily Trescowe."

"I know, and somehow I need to see Emily alone so I can apologize and try to make amends," Alex exclaimed. "Is there a certain time of day that Emily ..."

"Hello, Hugh, Mr. Spenser ... Alex." Emily felt as though she walked in on a serious discussion. "I'm just here to browse, as usual. Didn't mean to interrupt. I'll be quiet as a mouse." As she walked down to the end of the row of fiction, Alex looked at Hugh and Creighton with a look as if to say, "What luck!" Hugh and Creighton took the hint and disappeared into the back room so Alex could speak with Emily alone. No one else was in the shop at the moment, so Alex raced down the aisle to Emily.

"I need to speak to you, Emily. I need to apologize for what happened last night. My father's behavior was more than rude, and when he collapsed, I had to stay with him. I hope you understand. "

Emily looked at Alex with a puzzled frown. "There is no need for you to apologize, Alex. It wasn't your fault. I just don't understand why he spoke to me that way. He's never met me and yet, he seems to dislike me immensely. Do you know why?"

"I can't explain it, and when I tried to talk to him about it this morning, he just ignored my questions and changed the subject. From something he did say, I get the impression that he is not overly fond of any women, so I don't think his outrage was directed solely at you. I am so very sorry, Emily. I don't seem to have any influence on him, and his actions last night were unforgivable."

"Please don't blame yourself. He is your father and he loves you. Please don't let what happened damage your relationship with him. He needs you, and he is evidently trying to protect you from something. I'm just not sure what," Emily sighed.

"Thank you for understanding, Emily. I guess I missed my chance to walk with you in the rain." Alex took Emily's hand and smiled. She blushed profusely and stammered, "There will be other opportunities for that, I am sure."

Alex squeezed her hand as she let go and left the bookshop, forgetting what she went there for in the first place.

# CHAPTER 18

Joanna's funeral was set for the following Saturday. Polvenon Mine would pay for a small service and the burial. Many of the mine workers and their families would attend out of respect for the family of one of their own. No one had forgotten the death of Joanna's father two years earlier. To have another death in the same family so soon after was hard to take. The family would be taken care of by the wives of the mine workers until some type of work could be found for Mrs. Simmons to do at home that would bring in enough income to feed their little family of four. Alex Polvenon assured Mrs. Simmons that her rent would be paid until then.

On Saturday, the Trescowes, along with Kelly Rose and Tom, attended the funeral service at St. Stephen's Methodist Church in Polvenon Cove. Emily could see that it was difficult for Reverend Hawthorne to conduct a funeral service for one so young. After the service, Katherine ran to Emily and hugged her, tears falling freely but silently. It nearly broke Emily's heart. Norah invited all in attendance to Rumford Inn for some refreshments. Tudy had been up most of the night cooking and baking up a storm. As Mrs. Simmons sat with Norah and Emily at a table near the window, Emily noticed Alex walking up the path. She went out to greet him. "Hello, Alex."

"Hello, Emily. I won't be staying long as I gave my condolences to the family before the service. I just wanted to see how you were doing and ask if there was anything I could do." Emily knew that Alex would most likely not be welcomed by those inside as many of them blamed the Polvenons for this tragedy.

"No, Alex, I don't think so, but thank you for coming and thank you for offering."

Alex took Emily's hand in his own and squeezed it gently, then turned and left.

Emily stood there, watching him walk away and thinking that someday Alex would oversee the mines and things would change. She said a silent prayer that it would be so as she turned and walked back inside.

Later that day, Emily went down to the docks to sit, her feet dangling in the water, her nose in a book. Moments later, a shadow crossed over her. Startled, she looked up to find Ned Draper smiling down at her. "Hello, Emily. Beautiful day to be out in the fresh air, eh?" he said as he sat down next to her.

"Mr. Draper. What are you doing here? I thought you'd have gone back to Tremorna by now. Did the meeting go well last night?" Emily asked nervously, fidgeting in an effort to keep a little distance between them without being too obvious.

"The outcome of the meeting was everything I hoped it would be. I have not yet returned to Tremorna because I wanted to see you, Emily.

I find you very refreshing to talk to and enjoy your company immensely, what little there has been anyway."

"Th-thank you for saying so, Mr. Draper," Emily sputtered, uncomfortable with his forwardness.

"Please, Emily, call me Ned. Actually, I would like to invite you to the Truro Ball next month. It's the event of the year, and I would very much like you to be my guest. What do you say, Emily, would you like to go?"

Emily didn't know what to say. She'd never been to a ball before, especially as grand a one as the Truro Charity Ball. He was right; it was the biggest dance of the year in this area of Cornwall. She had always wondered if she would ever be invited to attend. Touched that he would ask, but still hesitant about the man himself, she didn't know what she should do. And then there was Alex, and all the confusion of the night before. If she were to go to such a ball, she had dreamed of going with someone like Alex.

"I am very honored by your invitation Mr....Ned; however, I will have to decline your offer. You see, I am in mourning for a very dear friend of mine, and it would not feel right somehow to attend a ball so soon after her death. I hope you understand."

"Oh, how rude of me. Of course. Mr. and Mrs. Trescowe told me about the Simmons girl. I should have offered you my condolences first, and I hope you will still accept them. But your parents seemed to think the ball would be just the thing to take your mind off such a tragedy. I do understand, Emily; perhaps another time."

"Wait, Mr....Ned," Emily said quietly, brushing tears from her eyes. "I appreciate your thoughtfulness. Thank you. I have changed my mind. I'd like to go to the ball. I believe it may do me some good after all. I had not looked at it that way. And it is a month away yet."

"Are you sure, Emily? I would make sure that you had a wonderful time—an evening you won't forget." Ned smiled, sensing that she had never been to an event as grand as this would be.

"Yes, Ned. I'll go with you. What time should I be ready?" Emily asked, still not sure if this was what she really wanted to do.

"My carriage will be at Rumford Inn by mid-afternoon. We will have dinner when we arrive at the ball, and the dancing begins as the sun sets. We must get you there early enough to have time to change into your gown." As Ned arose to leave, he thanked her, and as he turned to wave at Emily, he shouted, "Please tell Mr. and Mrs. Trescowe that you will be home by midnight!"

Emily nodded as she waved back. When she was alone again, she decided that she would make every effort to have a wonderful time at the ball. "I wonder if Alex will be there." Emily thought suddenly. In her excitement at that possibility, she practically skipped back home, forgetting all about her book.

"Oh, Kelly Rose! I never thought of that! Whatever am I going to wear?" Emily cried, as she stared wide-eyed into her wardrobe the next morning, a look of desperation on her face.

"Ah, well, that is a wee bit of a dilemma." Kelly Rose sighed as she plopped down on Emily's bed. "I do fancy myself quite a talent with a needle, but even I canna whip up a dress as fancy as you would need."

Emily sat glumly on the bed next to Kelly Rose, and Norah caught sight of two frowning faces as she passed Emily's room. "Why are you two looking so forlorn? You'd think t'wasn't a beautiful day at all."

"Oh, Norah! I hastily accepted an invitation from Mr. Draper to the charity ball in Truro, and I have nothing to wear."

Norah was taken aback a bit by this announcement. "Well, Emily, first of all, don't you think that Mr. Draper should have asked your father's permission before making such an offer?"

"But I thought Mr. Draper had ..." Emily was pondering why Ned had told her that he had already asked permission but decided not to say anything to Norah for now. Maybe she misunderstood him. Or was Ned being dishonest with her, and, if so, why?

"Well I have nothing to wear to a fancy ball, so maybe it's not such a good idea after all." Emily plopped down onto her bed, frustrated about the whole situation.

"I will talk to your father, Emily, and see what he has to say. I may just have a few ideas about a dress, but let's not worry about it until I've talked to Elliot.

# CHAPTER 19

With a spring in his step, Ned Draper thought he might stop in to see Philip Polvenon to let him know things were going swimmingly. Benjamin saw Ned coming and opened the door for him. "Good afternoon, Mr. Draper. Please come in. I will let Mr. Polvenon know that you are here. Is he expecting you?"

Ned strutted into the hall and, flinging his gloves off and waving them in the air, said, "No, he is not, but I am sure he will be glad to see me."

"Yes sir," Benjamin said, eyeing Mr. Draper suspiciously. As he left the room, Benjamin wondered why Philip would be glad to see this man as both Philip and Benjamin hadn't much use for him in the past. Nor did Alexander, for that matter.

As Philip entered the room, Ned practically ran to him, and with a big smile said, "Mr. Polvenon, my good man! So good to see you. I've come with wonderful news!"

"And what news could you possibly have that would be wonderful, Mr. Draper?" Philip snarled, ignoring Ned's outstretched hand.

Undeterred, Ned replied, "Sir, would you mind if we had a seat, preferably near the fire, as it's getting a bit nippy outside, and I've walked quite a way." Ned walked into Philip's study uninvited and took the chair nearest the fireplace. Philip grunted and sat opposite.

"So, what's the big news, Mr. Draper?"

"I have invited Miss Emily Trescowe to the Truro Ball, and she has accepted. It was simple, really."

"You what?!" Philip spat out so loudly that Ned jumped out of his chair. "Are you out of your mind? You don't just invite a lady, at her young age, to a ball without first getting permission from her father. What were you thinking?" Philip paced erratically as Ned followed him back and forth like a puppy. Philip stopped suddenly and shouted, "Do you know nothing of proper etiquette, you uncouth man? You've probably ruined any chance of taking Emily to the ball by your improper behavior. How are we going to fix this now?"

Trying to appease Philip, Ned quietly suggested that he go to Emily's father, profusely apologize for his behavior towards his daughter, beg his forgiveness, and put forth his invitation in the proper manner.

"What's done is done, Mr. Draper. Do you really think that slinking over there now to try to smooth things over will work with Elliot Trescowe? I think not! However, there is nothing for it but to try; hopefully, you will succeed. I never took you for a bumbling idiot, Ned Draper, but now I'm starting to wonder. Go, before I throw you out! Report back here as soon as the deed is done, and you had better be successful. Do I make myself clear?"

Without responding, Ned made a quick getaway before he made things worse. "What a temper Philip Polvenon has." he thought. "I've been told to watch my step around him, and now I see why."

Norah went downstairs to see if she could catch Elliot during a lull in his hectic evening and found, to her surprise, Ned Draper speaking to her husband. Elliot listened to the man for a while and then Norah heard him say, "Well, Mr. Draper, I appreciate you coming here to ask permission to take Emily to the ball. She is quite young, you know, and this would be her first ball. I see no reason not to approve, but with one stipulation. I hear that Hugh Spenser is taking Miss Fairfax to the ball, and I think it would be a good idea for the four of you to go together. I am sure that you are an honorable man, Mr. Draper, but we hardly know you, and I feel that Emily would feel more comfortable if Hugh and Miss Fairfax accompanied you."

"I am most certainly agreeable to that, Mr. Trescowe, especially if it puts your daughter at ease. How would I contact Mr. Spenser, sir?"

"He and his father run the only bookshop in the village. You can't miss it as it is called Spenser's Bookshop. It is a very old and respected establishment, and they are very good people. I am sure you will enjoy his company."

Feeling much more at ease about Emily attending the ball, Norah went immediately to the attic to find a trunk that she hadn't opened for years. It brought back so many memories as it was filled with clothes that had been worn by her sister Margaret who disappeared mysteriously about seventeen years ago. No one ever found out what happened to her. At the same time, the love of her life, Drake Monroe, also disappeared. It has always been Norah's hope that they ran away together and that someday she would hear news of them, but it had been so long now that she had given up hope.

Sighing, Norah began to pull dresses from the trunk. She remembered the beautiful ice blue gown that Margaret once wore to the Truro Ball. When she lifted it out and examined it, she found that it just needed freshening up, and a slight tear in the hem needed to be mended. Other than that, it was still as beautiful as it was so many years ago.

"I should be able to have this ready for the charity ball," Norah thought. "She will be so surprised. I can't wait to see the look on her face!"

As Norah worked on the dress, a tear fell from her eye as she remembered how beautiful her sister was. Margaret was a year older than Norah and was making plans with Drake for their wedding day at the time of her disappearance. They were so happy and then they were gone.

Norah finished repairing the tear and went down to the kitchen to lightly steam the wrinkles and hang it near an open window to freshen overnight. She closed her eyes for a moment and pictured Emily in the ice blue gown. "She will be as beautiful as Margaret was in it. Of that I am sure."

The next morning, Emily woke up to see the beautiful blue gown hanging on her bedroom door. "Oh! How deliciously lovely! Kelly Rose!" Emily shouted as Kelly Rose came running. "What is it, Miss Emily?" But there was already a smile in Kelly Rose's eyes as she knew what Norah had accomplished the night before.

"This is simply the most stunning gown I've ever seen. Where did it come from? You know something, don't you?" Emily laughed as she jumped from her bed to feel the soft chiffon to make sure it was real.

At that moment, Norah walked into the room. "Surprise! Do you like it?"

"I love it, Mother. Please tell me where it came from." Emily pleaded.

"It was my sister's gown, the one she wore to her first Truro Charity Ball eighteen years ago. I kept it in storage all these years, hoping someday someone would be able to wear it again. It's yours now, Emily. I want you to try it on so if any alterations need to be made, I can have them finished by the night of the ball."

"I don't know what to say," Emily whispered as she folded Norah into a crushing hug. "It's really beautiful, and I thank you. But wait, does this mean that Father gave his permission?"

"Yes, Mr. Draper was here later in the evening to seek Elliot's approval. He certainly has a way with words as he seemed to have won him over. You may attend the ball with Mr. Draper, and Hugh Spenser and Miss Fairfax will be accompanying you."

"Oh, I'm so glad! I still feel a little intimidated by Mr. Draper, so it will put me at ease knowing Hugh and Miss Fairfax will be coming along. Now I am really looking forward to it!" Emily crooned as she danced around the room, grabbing Kelly Rose for a waltz as Norah giggled and quietly left the room.

# CHAPTER 20

Emily woke up bright and early the next morning. She was going to walk to Helsted today to visit the Simmons family and bring them some of Tudy's sweetbreads. It would be the first time she visited since Joanna's funeral. Emily sighed heavily as she wondered what would become of the family and others like them.

As she stepped outside, Augie was sweeping the front stoop of the tavern. "Mornin', miss. 'Tis a fine day to be outdoors. And where you be off to?"

"Morning, Augie. It truly is a beautiful day, and I'm on my way to Helsted to visit the Simmons family."

"Oh, aye," Augie said quietly with his head down. " 'Tis a sad situation, that is, miss. Well, you give 'em my best. 'Tisn't a nicer family nor one more deservin' than they."

As they were conversing, Augie noticed Ned coming down the lane, probably from an early morning walk. "Steer clear of 'im, missy. He's a bad un."

"Why do you say that, Augie?" Emily looked puzzled.

"I say that as I've seen 'im struttin' to and fro 'tween 'ere and the manor house. Don't know what there would be for he to be talkin' with the master aboot, but e's up to no good, mark my words."

Ned didn't see Emily or Augie as he stepped into the inn. Emily started her walk to Helsted, perplexed by Augie's words. Why would Ned have anything to do with the Polvenons? Maybe he was their banker? But Augie made it sound like he visits there often. Maybe he is a friend of Alex. Well, Emily knew that whatever Augie says mustn't be taken too seriously.

Mrs. Simmons was in the yard hanging clothes out to dry. The younger children were scampering around her, trying to catch what looked like a chipmunk. Katherine was nowhere to be found as her shift as a bal maiden wouldn't be over until late, and then she had to walk home.

"Hello, Mrs. Simmons." Emily smiled.

"Oh, hello, Miss Emily," Mrs. Simmons exclaimed as she hung the last little shirt. "What brings you by? Come in, come in!" She shooed Emily into the kitchen.

"I brought a treat from Tudy. I know how much you enjoy her sweetbread," Emily said as she placed the breads on the table. "How have you been, Mrs. Simmons? Are the children okay? They seem healthy and happy."

"Oh, aye. But 'tis missin' their big sister something awful." Mrs. Simmons bowed her head to hide her bloodshot eyes. "Katherine is at the mine, and when she gets home, she's usually too tired to pay them any mind, so they are pretty much on their own."

Emily scanned the kitchen and the adjoining room as they talked. It looked as though there were bare spots on the walls and shelves, and when Mrs. Simmons noticed the sad look on Emily's face, she whispered, "I know, Miss Emily, but we have to eat, and I've bargained just about everything we own to put food on the table and keep them clothed as best I can. T'weren't much I could sell outright, but traded for food mostly.

Emily grew angrier when she saw how the Simmons were living. The hovel looked more disheveled and bare than ever before. Mrs. Simmons kept the place as neat and clean as she could, and Emily could smell something like watered-down stew cooking on the stove.

"I am so sorry, Mrs. Simmons, but this simply is too much to take!" Emily blurted out. "Did you receive any pay for Joanna's last day yet?"

Mrs. Simmons harrumphed, "No, child, and we most likely never will. Katherine works so hard, and she were hoping she would receive a pay raise to what Joanna was making as she's doing the work now, but they say she's too young, and they can't pay her more until she's at least thirteen. She be only just turned ten now."

After playing catch with the children for a little while, Emily said her goodbyes and told Mrs. Simmons she would try to talk to Mr. Alex to see if there was anything that could be done. She knew that Philip Polvenon would not budge an inch to help any of the miners, no matter what the circumstances, but Emily felt that it was worth a try to talk to his son, who seemed to empathize with their plight.

# CHAPTER 21

Alex strolled into the kitchen to grab a quick bite when he noticed Benjamin walking away from the back of the manor toward the woods. Again, he was carrying what looked like a satchel and a tray. More than curious by now, Alex followed at a distance. Soon he spotted Benjamin walking into the door of the abandoned cottage on the estate. No one had used it as long as Alex could remember. It was always declared haunted, and since Alex was a little boy, he never went near it as Benjamin used to tell such horrific ghost stories about it. As he grew older, he forgot all about it.

Alex waited outside, and when Benjamin walked out of the cottage and locked the door behind him, Alex stepped onto the path causing Benjamin to jump, dropping a full tray of food with a loud clatter. "So, this is where you go with all that food, clothing, and bedding. What's really going on here, Benjamin?" The tone of Alex's voice told Benjamin that he must tell the truth for once and damn the consequences. Philip would be livid, but it couldn't be helped. More lies would just get him into more trouble in the long run. He was so tired of keeping this secret—so weary of it all.

"Tell me now, Benjamin, or I will walk in there and find out for myself!" Alex started to walk toward the shabby little building and noticed that there were bars on the windows. "Why would there be bars on the windows, Benjamin?" His voice was raised to a high pitch now.

In an effort to regain his composure, Benjamin stood tall and stated simply, "Yes, Alex. It's time you know the truth. If you would come into the kitchen and have a seat, I will make some tea and try to explain everything, but please promise me that you will remain calm and let me tell the whole story before you say anything."

As impatient as Alex was to get to the bottom of this mystery, he could see that Benjamin was quite shaken. He promised to listen without interruptions.

Emily was staking the leaning red hollyhocks, still pondering the mystery around Ned when Mr. Terwilliger's cart could be heard clanking down the lane.

"Well if that isn't a beautiful sight! Hello, Miss Emily. Can I interest you in any lace, ribbons, buttons, bootlaces?"

"Hello, Mr. Terwilliger. No. I have no need of those today, but thank you kindly. I am looking for a small gift for Norah though, as she is working so hard to get my dress ready for the charity ball. Do you have any ideas?"

"Well, I think I have just the thing, Miss Emily. I have brought with me a small, beautifully embossed book of poetry. It is an "antho ... antho...,"

"Anthology?"

"Why yes, that's the word ... of American authors. Is that something you think she would enjoy?"

"Oh, yes! That's perfect." As Emily was paying for her purchase, Mr. Terwilliger, always one for idle talk, said, "So, the charity ball, eh? Is that handsome Mr. Alex taking you? Or maybe Hugh Spenser?"

Emily laughed, knowing that he liked to pass along juicy tidbits of gossip as he made his rounds. "Neither, Mr. Terwilliger." It suddenly dawned on Emily that if anyone knew anything about Ned Draper, it would certainly be Mr. Terwilliger. "Actually, Mr. Ned Draper has asked me to the ball."

Mr. Terwilliger looked up sharply. "Ned Draper, you say?"

"Do you know him?"

"Oh, I know of him, Miss Emily. I hear a lot of things on my travels from village to village, and I can't say that I've ever heard anything good about the man. I've never met him, but from what I've heard, he's a shady character and not to be trusted. Oh, Miss Emily. Do be careful!"

"Don't worry, Mr. Terwilliger; we will be attending the ball with Hugh and his lady friend. There will be no opportunity for any inappropriateness."

"Still, I'd feel better if you were going with someone the likes of young Mr. Alex. Well, see that you stay close to Hugh; if need be, he'll see you right. Got to go now, Miss Emily. You take care now."

Emily was starting to have a bad feeling about Mr. Ned Draper. "Oh, if only Alex would have invited me to the ball instead!"

# CHAPTER 22

B enjamin spoke in a rush as if he had to get it all out before he lost his nerve.

"When your mother, Alexa, died, your father was devastated. He began to lash out at everyone and everything. A few months later, he met another woman. She quickly became an obsession, so much so it drove her away. She was younger than he was, and she had so much life in her. I think your father fed off that, for a while at least. It soon became obvious to him that she was not interested in him as a suitor. Rumors reached him that she was seeing someone and had fallen in love." Benjamin paused and sighed. He remembered how Philip took the news.

"As you can imagine, your father was livid. He wanted this woman all to himself. If he couldn't have her, no one would have her. You must understand, Alex, your father had just lost his wife, the love of his life, and this new woman came into his life so soon after, that he just replaced her, in his mind, with Alexa. One day, Philip was walking in the backwoods when he heard laughter coming from the old cottage. In his anger that someone was having a tryst on his property, he slammed open the front door of the cottage and found this woman with her lover.

In a fit of violence, he beat the man to death with a shovel. I later found out that the man was a notorious smuggler the riding officers had been searching for."

"I'll never forget that day. Your father came running into the manor, blinded by tears and rage. He begged me to help him. I followed him into the woods and saw the smuggler's body lying at the edge of the path." Benjamin shuddered, remembering the gruesomely bloody scene. "We buried him in the woods, Alex," Benjamin whispered, shaking his head. "Since that day, your father never let the woman leave the cottage; he put crude bars on the windows and locked the doors from the outside so she couldn't leave. He's had her locked up there for over seventeen years! No one has been to see her but me," he cried. "I've often wondered if you ever thought it odd that your father never hired a cook or a cleaning woman. I was the only one he could trust. He made me swear to keep his secret—all these years." Benjamin sobbed. "I'm so sorry, Alex. I wanted to tell you so many times, but I was afraid that your father … well, you've seen him when he's in a rage. There's no telling what he'd do."

Alex wanted to say something, ask questions, shout—anything! He could not believe what he was hearing. But then Benjamin continued. "There's more, Alex. About a month after the poor smuggler's death, the woman told me she was with child. When I spoke to Philip about this, he told me to 'get rid of the wretched thing as soon as it's born.' The child, a girl, was born without complications. The poor woman sobbed hysterically when I took the child to the orphanage. I left her on the doorstep, Alex! On the doorstep! I can't believe I ever could have done that, but I didn't see any other way. Philip didn't want the 'bastard child' anywhere on the premises. And the orphanage couldn't know where she came from."

"The baby's mother became despondent after that. She's been that way for all these years. She eats only enough to sustain her. She doesn't talk to me, only stares out the window at the woods. The only fresh air she ever gets is when I open the door while I am there with her. He won't even let me take her for a walk in the woods."

After a long pause, Alex finally drew a breath and looked at Benjamin. "I don't even know what to make of this, Benjamin. What you've told me—it's so outlandish! So unbelievable! I'm having a difficult time making any sense of it. So, you've been keeping this from everyone all these years? What a horrible burden for you, keeping such a dark, horrid secret. You say she doesn't speak, Benjamin. Does she show any indication that she knows you are there when you visit her?"

"No, Master Alex. She won't even eat when I am there. I leave a tray there, and when I go back to deliver her next meal, she's barely eaten a bite. When I can, I spend time with her, telling her of things that are going on in the village, mentioning names of people she may have known, but she barely blinks—just stares."

"Benjamin, I notice that you haven't mentioned the lady's name."

"It's because I promised your father never to mention her name to anyone."

Philip had been standing in the entrance for just a few seconds when he overheard the last part of the conversation. "My God, Benjamin! What have you done?" Alex twisted around just in time to see his father fall to the ground. Benjamin jumped up and ran to Philip. It was obvious to both Alex and Benjamin that Philip was having one of his spells. This time it was more serious as he was having trouble speaking, his words coming out in broken sentences. Philip glared at Benjamin and pointed, "You f-fool. I should have n-never ... trusted ..." Alex could see that his father was having difficulty breathing. He placed a pillow under his head and asked Benjamin to help carry him to his bed.

"No! Leave ... me alone." Philip pushed Benjamin away as forcefully as he could. He stared into Alex's eyes and grabbed at his hand. "L-loved her! She ... betrayed ..."

Alex tried to calm his father. He could see he was failing. "Father, try to—"

"No! M-my fault, n-not Benjamin ... forgive me...." As Philip began to slip away, his last word came as a faint whisper. "Mar ..."

# CHAPTER 23

Philip Polvenon's funeral was attended by all the townspeople, rich and poor, young and old. Some had never even met the man but went out of respect for what he'd done for the mining industry in that area. They didn't always agree with his methods, but no one could say he didn't get things done. Besides, there was to be a huge spread at Rumford Inn for all who attended, and who could pass up the opportunity to fill their stomachs and, for some, their pockets?

Alexander had taken a step back for a while from the condolences and good wishes of the people of Polvenon Cove. He walked up to the cliff path, needing time alone to think. He and Benjamin had managed to settle the woman into one of the bedrooms in the manor house, and although she still would not speak, she seemed to be eating a little more each day. She also had taken to Alex and had even let him guide her on a tour of the place she would be calling home for the unforeseeable future. "Once she gets on her feet, I will prod Benjamin for more information about her." Alex decided. "He seems reluctant still to mention her name and refers to her as 'lady,' as have I. My father must have really put the fear of God in poor Benjamin. For now, it's essential that we get her well again."

Alex went back to Rumford Inn only to be met by an eager crowd of miners, wanting to know what would happen to their jobs. Alex reassured them that their jobs were safe for now and that he would be taking a hard look at what changes may need to be made. Seemingly satisfied, the minors started to drift off. Alex looked for Emily, but she was nowhere to be found.

Emily had been so busy in the kitchen that she had no time to convey her sympathies to Alex. Tudy and Emily were preparing parcels of food to give to the miners and their families. Norah suggested they go up to the manor house the next day as there would be enough food left over to take to Alex and Benjamin.

"Did you happen to see Mr. Draper today?" Emily asked Norah. "I know that he knew the Polvenons, but I didn't see him at the funeral, and he hasn't been here for the meal either."

"I didn't see him, but maybe he was just a business associate of the Polvenons?"

"Even so." Emily wondered.

When Alex came home, he walked into the dining room, and Benjamin was just setting a plate in front of the woman. Both Alex and Benjamin had decided earlier to talk to her and relate to her the doings of their days in the hopes that someday she might open up and speak to them.

It was a small miracle that Benjamin was able to coax her to come down to the dining room for her meals. When she looked up and saw Alex, a brief smile passed her lips and it made Alex's day.

Later, when she went to bed for the night, Benjamin and Alex sat a while in front of the fire. "I'm sorry you were not able to attend Father's funeral, Benjamin."

"I know, Master Alex, but someone had to stay with the poor lady. She's comfortable with me, but I have noticed that she is warming up to you lately, which is good. Still, I think it would be a good idea if she had some female companionship, don't you?"

"Yes, I think that would be good for her. Any suggestions?"

Benjamin smiled. "Well, Master Alex, maybe this would be a good opportunity for you to invite Miss Emily for a visit. It may go a long way to repairing the damage done from her earlier confrontation with your father."

"You know, that is a splendid idea!" He winked at Benjamin. He was feeling better already.

# CHAPTER 24

Norah and Kelly Rose had so much to clean up the day after the funeral that Norah thought it best that at least Emily make an appearance at the manor as she didn't get a chance to talk to Alex yesterday. She took as many parcels of food as she could carry by herself. It wasn't a far walk. She remembered the last time she walked this path; it was when she ran home in the pouring rain the night that she ended up at the manor because of the storm. Philip Polvenon had looked at her so strangely and then collapsed right in front of her. "He must have been ill back then already," Emily thought. Poor Alex. His father was a tyrant, but he was still his father and must have loved him very much.

Emily reached the manor and rapped at the imposing front door. Benjamin opened it and exclaimed with surprise, "Why, Miss Emily! How nice to see you. Come in, come in. Here, let me take those."

"Hello, Benjamin; it's good to see you. These are the leftovers from yesterday. I am sorry that I didn't get a chance to talk to you then, but we were very busy in the kitchen."

"Well, Miss Emily, I was not able to make it to the funeral. I had ... something to attend to."

"Emily!" Alex rushed down the stairs as soon as he heard her voice. "Have you come for a visit? Please come into the drawing room, and I'll stoke the fire. Benjamin, would you take Emily's coat and bring us some tea?"

"Certainly, Master Alex, I'll put the tea on and get these wonderful parcels put away."

Emily sat in the same chair that was offered to her on her first visit. "I wanted to give you my condolences, Alex. I am sure this has not been an easy time for you."

"Thank you, Emily. I appreciate that. Yesterday was a difficult day. It was kind of Norah and Elliot to open Rumford Inn's doors to those who attended. Please let them know how grateful I am for all that they did and that I will reimburse them very soon."

"Oh, I don't think that will be necessary, Alex; they do not expect recompense. It is something they wanted to do for you."

They enjoyed each other's company as Benjamin served them tea. After a short while, Emily felt it was time to leave and stood. "I really should be going. I left Norah and Kelly Rose with quite a mess. If there is anything I can do for you, please don't hesitate to ask."

Alex looked at Benjamin and Benjamin nodded to him. "Well, Emily, if you have a few minutes, I do have a favor to ask."

Elliot stalked into the kitchen and, amidst the disarray, shouted, "Well, the nerve of that man! If he weren't already long gone, I'd run him out of Polvenon Cove myself!"

Norah looked wide-eyed at Elliot, not remembering a time when he was so riled. "What happened, Elliot, and what man are you talking about?"

"It seems that Mr. Ned Draper has left the inn without paying for his stay. He did not appear for breakfast this morning and, as you know, he was not at the funeral yesterday. I knocked on his door just now, and it was open a crack, so I walked in. He is gone, along with all of his belongings."

"Oh, dear!" cried Kelly Rose. "What about the Truro Charity Ball? Whatever will Miss Emily say! Oh, Norah, I knew there was something about that man I didn't trust."

Norah remembered how excited Emily was to be attending the ball. The anticipation had brought her out of her grief over losing her best friend. "Now calm down, both of you. There must be an explanation. Maybe he had to leave unexpectedly due to an emergency."

"If that were the case, would he have taken all of his things?" Elliot plopped onto a chair dejectedly. "I hope I never see his face again." After calming himself down a bit, he looked up at Norah and asked, "Would you like me to talk to Emily?"

"No, dear. Thank you, but I think she will take it better from me. She will be home soon. I will tell her then." Elliot stood and hugged Norah and said, "I'm going for a walk—a long one."

Alex explained to Emily that Benjamin had befriended a woman who, it seems, is without a home. "She is staying here for the time being.

Benjamin thinks she would benefit from some female companionship." Emily was only too happy to oblige. "I will speak with Norah and see if there might be a time soon for us to visit with her."

Norah's motherly instincts emerged as soon as Emily explained the situation to her. "I think that we should make some time tomorrow to visit with her. The poor woman. I wonder how Benjamin met her."

"Alex didn't go into much detail, unfortunately. Kelly Rose and I were going to go to the grocer's tomorrow morning, but we could go later." Norah smiled. She didn't know if Emily was more excited to meet this woman or see Alex.

"There is something I need to speak to you about, Emily. Please sit down." Emily grabbed a blueberry scone and sat at the kitchen table. Norah placed a teapot between them and sighed. "I'm afraid Mr. Draper has left us. His room is empty."

Puzzled, Emily asked, "Did he leave a note for me?"

"No, Emily. Elliot and I looked. He left no note, and he left without paying for his room and board."

"Oh no! I'm so sorry. I wonder what could have happened." Suddenly remembering, Emily cried, "Oh, Norah, my dress! The ball!"

That evening, Kelly Rose knocked on Emily's bedroom door. "Come in."

"Miss Emily, Norah told me about Mr. Draper. Now I know how disappointed you must be about missing the ball, but I for one, am glad that he is gone. I never liked the man and was worried for your safety. I didn't say anything earlier because you were so excited about going and it was so good to see you happy again."

"You know, Kelly Rose, I am actually relieved. I never really wanted Ned to take me. I guess I was willing to overlook his arrogance because I so wanted to go to the ball."

"He was rather a snob!" Kelly Rose exclaimed. Emily looked up at Kelly Rose, and they both burst into laughter. "You always know just what to say, Kelly Rose."

# CHAPTER 25

Bright and early the next morning, Kelly Rose and Emily made their trip to the grocer's, and when they got back to the inn, Norah was ready and waiting to visit Polvenon Manor. Emily had told Norah all that Benjamin had shared about the woman he befriended. "I wonder what this woman is like, how old she is, how she met Benjamin. Oh, I am so full of questions!" Norah exclaimed excitedly.

"Well, I think you need to temper your enthusiasm as it may scare her away." Emily laughed.

Benjamin answered their knock and invited them in. As they stood in the vast hallway, Benjamin took their wraps and told them that Alex would be with them in a moment. Before he could invite them into the drawing room, Norah looked up and saw Alex descending the stairs with a woman on his arm. She started to walk towards the woman, never taking her eyes off her. "Oh, my God! Margaret? It can't ... but how ... is it really you?"

The woman was startled by Norah's exuberance. But there was something about her that was familiar. "I know this woman," Margaret thought. As she and Alex slowly reached the bottom of the stairs, Norah could see confusion and fear on her beautifully familiar face.

"Margaret, it's me ... your sister, Norah." By now, Norah was sobbing into her hands. The woman walked up to her and gently pulled her hands away from her face. She spoke for the first time. "Norah ..." and they fell into each other's arms, hugging each other tightly and crying tears of unrestrained joy!

Wiping tears away from his own eyes, Benjamin suggested they all go into the dining room. Norah sat next to Margaret, not wanting to let her out of her sight for a minute. "I just can't believe it! After all these years! Where did you go, Margaret? What happened to you? How did you get here? Why didn't you let us know?"

Margaret pulled away slightly, confused by all the questions. Alex stepped in and said, "Norah, I am just as shocked as you are to find out that this woman—Margaret—is your sister. I am sure that Benjamin is just as surprised." Alex looked up at Benjamin and Benjamin replied, "If I'd only known. I am so sorry. This is all my fault."

"No, Benjamin, this was my father's doing. You did his bidding and cared for this woman regardless of his threats. I think it is time to tell the whole story."

Mr. Terwilliger made his weekly stop at Rumford Inn just as Elliot and Tom Stone were going over supplies that had just been delivered. "Hello, Mr. Trescowe, Tom."

"Hello to you, Mr. Terwilliger," Tom shouted as he carried bundles into the inn.

"I heard a tidbit next village over that your Mr. Draper has up and left without a word."

Elliot stopped what he was doing and stared at Mr. Terwilliger. "What have you heard? That scoundrel left us without paying!"

"Well, I 'eard he was in Spider Pub, drinkin' and spilling 'is guts. Seems as though 'e were workin' for Master Polvenon. 'E was going to get a large chunk of money from 'im for keepin' your Miss Emily occupied and away from his son, Alex. When Mr. Draper found out Master Polvenon ... passed, 'e up and left in a hurry, hoping no one would find out 'bout their dirty doings. Glad to see the back of 'im, I am. Feel bad for Miss Emily but, ball or no ball, she's better off rid of the likes of 'im."

By the time Benjamin had answered all of Norah's questions and related the story of Drake Monroe's death, Margaret's baby, and his care of Margaret over the years, Alex and Benjamin left the three women to themselves for a while.

Norah was slowly coming around to the fact that Margaret was really here. Margaret had so many questions for Norah and gradually spoke for the first time in many years. She kept looking at Emily, and when Norah noticed, she exclaimed, "Oh Margaret! In all this excitement I haven't even introduced you to my daughter. Margaret, this is Emily."

Margaret stared at Emily. "Emily," she said quietly. "That is what I named my daughter—Emily."

Norah looked at Emily and then at Margaret. Suddenly it all came together. "Margaret, Elliot and I adopted Emily from the Tremorna Orphanage when she was four years old! C-could she possibly be your Emily?"

Emily was awestruck! Can this be?

Margaret stood up and walked over to Emily. "I remember ... Benjamin—I gave him a yellow blanket to wrap her in." Now Emily stood, tears rolling unchecked down her face. She looked at Margaret and whispered, "I still have that blanket."

# CHAPTER 26

The next morning, the sun shimmered on the wet cliff path as it had rained the night before. Drops of dew were still on the pink sea thrift, and the waters below were calm as glass. As Alex and Emily walked along to their favorite bench, they discussed the revelations of the day before.

"I still can't believe it, Alex. I never thought I would ever get to meet my real mother and now she's here!"

"It is awful what my father put her through all those years, but Benjamin took very good care of her during that time. She seems to be coming around and even joked with Benjamin this morning during breakfast."

"I am so glad to hear that, Alex. Mother is ecstatic about having her sister back in her life. And I have two wonderful mothers to love. Oh, Alex, pinch me! I don't think I could be happier if I tried!"

Alex took Emily's hand in his and turned her face toward his. "Miss Emily Trescowe, would you do me the honor of attending the Truro Charity Ball with me?"

"Oh, Alex, I would love to!" Emily jumped up. "And I have just the dress!"

As Alex pulled up in the Polvenon carriage, Emily had just made her entrance, descending the staircase in a cloud of ice blue. Margaret was present to witness Emily in her gown. "Oh, Emily!" Margaret cried. "I remember it well! You look stunning in it! All eyes will be on you tonight."

"As they were on you, Margaret, the night you wore it to the ball." Norah had a faraway look in her eyes, remembering that special night— the night when Drake Monroe swept her sister off her feet.

A knock on the inn door interrupted their private musings. Elliot went to the door and invited Alex inside. Alex saw Emily and practically swooned. He bowed to her and took her arm. As they walked to the carriage, Alex leaned over and whispered in her ear, "You take my breath away, my beautiful Emily."

The charity ball was everything Emily had hoped for, and more. Alex never left her side the entire evening. Emily was enchanted by all the colorful ball gowns—luscious yellows, gorgeous emerald greens, and the palest of lavenders. Alex assured her she was by far the most stunning woman in the room, and she laughed up at him while they twirled around the ballroom floor.

During a break in the music, Alex excused himself, telling Emily he would be right back. Puzzled and feeling a little uncomfortable in a room full of strangers, Emily's eyes followed Alex as he made his way to the bandstand. He climbed the few steps, cleared his throat, and said, "May I have your attention please. Thank you all for coming tonight. It is my honor to announce that the proceeds of this year's charity ball will be going to the families of the miners who have lost their lives working under the deplorable conditions of Polvenon Mine. An amount will also be set aside to establish a fund for injured miners unable to work so that they can continue to support their families while they get the medical help they need. So please, give generously!" Loud cheers and thunderous applause followed. As Alex stepped down, men shook his hand appreciatively, and women hugged him. The band struck a tune, and dancing continued well into the night.

Tucked snuggly into the Polvenon family carriage, Emily shivered as Alex sat down beside her, wrapping her in his arms to keep her warm. "I will never forget this night, Alex. Everything was so perfect."

Alex looked deep into Emily's blue eyes and whispered, "It is you who is perfect, my dear sweet Emily. And I love you—so much." When he kissed her, Emily knew that she would love this man until the day she died.

# EPILOGUE

Hugh Spenser and Kelly Rose were attendants at the wedding of Alexander Polvenon and Emily Trescowe. A year later, Kelly Rose married her longtime beau, Tom Stone. Being her matron-of-honor when in her eighth month proved to be quite a feat for Emily Polvenon. Both weddings were followed by a celebration at Rumford Inn, hosted by Elliot and Norah. Margaret, who now lived at the inn, made Emily's wedding gown, which was altered a year later for Kelly Rose.

Kelly Rose and Tom stayed on at Rumford Inn. They now have a two-year-old boy, Ian, and another child coming in a few months. Emily and her son, Jonathan, visit often, and her bond with both Margaret and Norah grows stronger every day.

Benjamin retains his duties at Polvenon Manor. Katherine Simmons continues her education and now lives at Polvenon Manor as Benjamin's assistant doing laundry, dishes, and fixing the occasional meal. The bars and locks have been taken off the little cottage in the back-woods. Emily and Alex have fixed it up and furnished it, and the Simmons family lives there now.

Working conditions at Polvenon Mine have greatly improved, and medical care is being provided to all miners and their families.

Emily and Alex still take their favorite walk along the footpath in the evenings when all has settled. As they look up at the stars, they thank God for all the blessings they've been given. And as they look down on the village, the lights of Rumford Inn burn brightly.